INJUSTICE SERVED

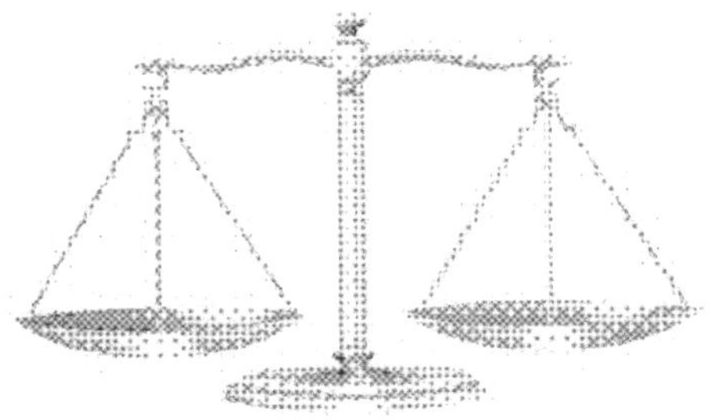

By

Robert Smits

<u>DEDICATIONS</u>

To the family who's real life experience, inspired me to write this book.

To my children, Carrie and John who's personal and professional accomplishments have always given me inspiration.

To all the men and women in law enforcement, who continuously fight the day to day battles, in the war on drugs, that some say can never be won, and who give inspiration to so many of us.

And finally, to my wife Linda, who humored my indulgence while I was writing it.

TABLE OF CONTENTS

PREFACE

In the year 2000, the estimated number of Marijuana Grow Ops in British Columbia, was estimated to be as high as 17,500. Numbers of that magnitude suggest, that exports are worth nearly 2 billion dollars. *

Sometimes innocent people get caught up in the law enforcement efforts to curb production, use, and export of drugs. When these events happen, it places both law enforcement and judicial systems, in compromising situations, and sets off chains of events, that no one would think possible. Justice isn't always served.

- *Excerpt from "Marijuana Growth in British Columbia", written by Stephen Easton, published by the Fraser Institute, May 2004*

CHAPTER ONE

The office was virtually dark, except for the dim light emitted by the lone hundred watt incandescent bulb, hanging bare from the ceiling. Just as well, there wasn't much to see in the twenty by twenty foot office of Jackson Walker, or Jake, as those close to him better knew him as. A desk, a filing cabinet, and a couple of tufted leather armchairs were all he really needed. Jake was six one, two hundred pounds with a fairly muscular build that came naturally. At forty-eight, he still had a thick, full head of hair. All in all, he was a good-looking man, in a rugged kind of way. A look that never had a problem attracting the ladies, but his dedication to his job, had given him little time for a social life. He had only been a private investigator a few short weeks, and was wondering if he could even make a go of it on his own. Jake couldn't help but question, whether he had made a huge mistake by leaving his job in corporate security, with a large, prestigious tech firm. The work was getting mundane and wasn't fulfilling…well he really didn't know what was missing in his life, but he knew there was a void that wasn't being filled. If it weren't for the six-figure salary he was pulling down, he would have left long ago. His new digs on Water Street near Abbott were in the trendy Gastown area of Vancouver, but the red brick façade of the two-story building that housed his office, was just that, a façade. The interior didn't live up to the upscale exterior, and was still in the restoration stage. Parts of it were still a construction zone. His office was on the second floor, and looked out over Water Street. In spite of it all, he was happy with the location. Surrounded by bars and restaurants, and even more importantly, a Starbucks only a block away. He had everything he needed, within a few minutes walk.

It was six thirty, and he could hear the whistle from the old Gastown Steam

Clock, as the June sun was just starting to drop from the western sky. Jake was just writing up the final report of his last case, surveillance of a cheating husband. The wife's lawyer had hired him, and even though he found these types of investigations distasteful, for now, it paid the bills. He was startled by a knock at the door, which then opened as a tall man, thirtyish, slim build, walked in. "Are you Mr. Walker?" the man asked. "I am, and Jake will be just fine." "My name is Steven Compton and I'm not sure what to do." Jake looked him up and down sizing him up, just like he did with most people he met for the first time. He pegged the man as somewhat reserved, but with a likeable manner about him. Jake replied, "Well, for starters take a seat and tell me what seems to be your problem?" "My father and mother are sitting in the Friday Harbor jail after being arrested by U.S. Customs, for smuggling drugs." "I think what you really need is a lawyer." "Yes, and that will be my first stop when I leave here." Steven was showing visible signs of stress now. "If you knew my parents, you would understand how ridiculous these charges are. What I need most is an investigator, to find out exactly what happened." "They're both in their late sixties, and I don't how well they can handle this. Dad's already had one heart attack, and this isn't doing anything to promote his recovery." "Ok" Jake said, "I'll take a preliminary look into it, and see what, if anything, I can do." "My fee is two hundred dollars an hour against a five thousand dollar retainer, plus expenses. Are you ok with that?" Steven agreed and wrote a cheque.

CHAPTER TWO

"Well, we're on the clock now so lets get started. First off, what are their names, and what exactly happened?" "Frank and Margaret. They had just recently bought a used, Catalina thirty foot sailboat, and this was supposed to be their shakedown cruise" "For the past six weeks they kept it moored at Thunderbird Marina in West Vancouver while they cleaned it up, and fitted it out." "Where exactly were the drugs found?" "According to dad, they found marijuana in the keel of the sailboat." "I don't know how much." "Where was the boat purchased?" Steven replied "From a police auction...ironic." Jake asked him if he knew the background on how it got into the auction, and he replied "no." "Ok" he said, "tomorrow I'll head down to Friday Harbor, and see what I can find out from U.S. customs." "In the mean time who will be representing them?" "I was going to call the lawyer I use for my business dealings." Jake told Steven that it was certainly his choice, but "in my experience, corporate lawyers generally don't have much expertise when it comes to criminal matters." Steven responded that he was open to suggestions. Jake wrote the name Carla Rossi, followed by a phone number, on the back of his business card, and handed it to Steven. Steven returned the gesture with one of his own cards, and they said their goodbyes.

Jake locked up the office for the night, and headed for the parking garage. He found his car, a cherry red nineteen sixty-three Jaguar XKE with a black convertible top. It was only the six cylinder, but it didn't matter, no one was going anywhere fast in the lower mainland anyway. He was proud of his car. It was one of only two indulgences, the other being Louis XIII cognac. As he drove towards the west end, where his condo was located, he couldn't help but wonder if he should have disclosed his relationship with Carla, when he referred Steven to her. No, he decided, she was a great criminal lawyer, and that's all that really mattered.

The next morning Jake awoke to clear skies, with a light breeze. He decided he would fly to Friday Harbor. Jake had a private pilots licence, with about a thousand hours of flight time. He owned a Cessna 182, which he kept at Boundary Bay airport. It was about thirty minutes further south than Vancouver International, but the difference in landing, and tie down fees, made it well worth the extra time getting there. He was about half way across the Arthur Lang Bridge, spanning the north arm of the Fraser River, when his phone rang. The female voice on the other end said "Jesus, if you're going to give out my private cell number, at least tell them not to call before seven." Jake was sure he heard a muted chuckle in the background. "Good morning to you too Carla, and you're welcome." "Seriously, your client called first thing and gave me the abridged version, then suggested I contact you," she answered. "I'm heading to Friday Harbor now, do you have time to join me?" "I'll call my assistant and have her juggle my schedule." "Great" Jake said, "meet me at the plane as soon as you can get there. I'll bring you up to speed, on the flight down. Don't forget your passport." He gave her directions, and Carla told him she was on her way.

By the time Carla arrived, Jake had completed his walk around, and filed his flight plan. He was always happy to see her. She was about five foot eight, average build, and above average figure, with a very attractive face, framed by raven shoulder length hair. She was Jakes senior by a year. They had known each other for about fifteen years. This would be the first time they would work together professionally. He remembered the first time they met. It was in court. Carla was representing a client he had caught stealing from the tech firm he worked at. After Jake testified, he stayed in the gallery for the remainder of the trial. She got her client off, but Jake was so impressed with her professionalism, that he didn't hold a grudge and he asked her out for a drink, when the trial was over. They were both married to other people at the time, so that's as far as it went. Over the years they'd stayed in touch, and when they both wound up divorced, for being more obsessed with their careers, than their marriages, they became friends with benefits. This seemed to work well for them both. Neither marriage produced any children.

When she arrived at the plane, they hugged, and Jake gave her a quick kiss hello, before they got in, and started the engine. When the run up was complete, he got his clearance from ground control, and taxied for runway 25. Winds were light so he calculated the thirty-eight mile flight, would take them about twenty minutes.

As soon as they were airborne, Jake climbed to three thousand feet, and brought Carla up to speed, with the details he had so far. She told him she had contacted the Friday Harbor Sheriffs department first thing, and was told the couple was scheduled for arraignment this afternoon. Now they could relax and enjoy the flight. For all the times he had flown over the Gulf and San Juan Islands, Jake never tired of the view, and Carla could understand why. After fifteen minutes Jake dialed up the local weather, and contacted Friday Harbor traffic, with his position and ETA. He set up for a right hand downwind for runway three four. When they touched down, they taxied to the customs shed and checked in. Jake called a cab, and they drove the short distance to the sheriffs department. It was Carla's turn to start earning her fee. She spoke with the deputy, and got a copy of the arrest report. From there, she was escorted to an interview room, and waited for the Compton's to be brought in.

When Frank and Margaret came in to the room and took their seats, the deputy left, and closed the door behind him. Carla could see that they were both under a lot of stress, and they looked as though they hadn't slept for days. Frank came across as reserved, just short of shy. Margaret was the opposite, she appeared quite excitable. After introductions were made Carla read them the charge *"Importation of a controlled schedule 1 substance (cannabis)"* and asked if they understood the charge. They both nodded yes. "Ok," Carla said in a calming voice, "as best as you can remember, tell me what happened. Also, do you mind if I record this, so I don't miss any details." They both agreed, and Frank began relating the events that led up to where they were now.

The two of them had left Thunderbird Marina around eight o'clock the previous morning, planning a weeklong cruise through the San Juan Islands. Everything was going great. Winds were light and the boat shook out well, giving them an extremely smooth sail all the way. At about four o'clock, they had made the mouth of Friday Harbor, dropped sail, and motored up to the customs shed, at the south end of the marina. Frank went ashore to the office, while Margaret stayed aboard. When Frank checked in with the CBP agent, the two of them, and a K9 handler with his service dog, returned to the boat. "While the first agent worked through a questionnaire with Margaret and me, the K9 handler led his dog through the boat. It was only a minute or two, and the K9 sat and barked, scratching at the cabin sole. It was at that point the agent asking the questions, told us to stand up, and he escorted us off the boat and back up to the office." He continued, explaining that after about thirty minutes, the K9 officer returned to the office, pulled his partner aside and spoke to him. "At that point they came over, read us our rights, and said they were charging us with importing drugs. We tried to explain that we had just purchased the boat, and knew nothing about any drugs. This didn't seem to impress them. They finger printed us, and put us in separate rooms." Frank continued, "Then they put us in handcuffs, and escorted us to a police car, where he drove us to the Sheriffs office. They took our photos and finger printed us again, then put us in cells." Margaret interjected "shortly after that they came to the cells and said we could each make a phone call." Frank jumped back in, "that's when I called Steven." Carla asked them if they were being treated ok, and if they needed anything. They indicated they were fine, but Carla could tell they were scared. A normal reaction. She turned off the recorder, and explained to them that they were going to be arraigned that afternoon, and that the first step, was get them released on bail. She also added, that they didn't have to worry about her fees, because Steven was taking care of them. Carla stood up and said "I'll see you in court in a couple of hours. Try to relax if you can." "Oh, Steven also hired and investigator, a Jake Walker, do I have your permission to share any information we discuss with him?" They both nodded yes without hesitation. With that she knocked on the interview room door, and the deputy let her out.

CHAPTER THREE

Jake was waiting, when Carla left the Sheriffs office. "Well…?" he asked. They're certainly scared, but that's to be expected. Let's go for lunch, and I'll go over their statement with you." "Way ahead of you. While you were in with the Compton's, I scoped out the local scene. There's a café called Millie's, just a block from here that looks pretty nice." "Lead on." Carla answered. The short walk down Second Street, to Millie's, gave them a chance to catch up on their personal lives. They hadn't seen each other for a couple of months, but it seemed like just yesterday. The two of them just appeared to click on every level. Jake couldn't help but wonder, if they had married each other all those years ago, if they would still be married. He shook it off immediately. If it isn't broke, don't try to fix it.

They arrived at Millie's and got a table right away. The restaurant was in an old converted house, that exuded a charm, appropriate for the island. Carla ordered the Chef's Salad and a glass of Merlot. Jake had the steak sandwich and just a Diet Coke, as he still had to fly them home. While they waited for their meals to arrive, Carla related the main points of her interview with the Compton's. She didn't have many details of the actual arrest, from the Sheriff, but would speak to the prosecutor before court. "Once the prosecutor lays out the states case, I'll have a better idea of what strategy we can pursue." The rest of lunch was spent in small talk, and more catching up. By the time they had finished, it was just before one o'clock. Jake paid the check, and they walked the short block and a half, back up Second Street to Court Street, where the combination courthouse, and town hall, were housed, kitty corner from the Sheriff's station.

They got there just as the clerk was opening the doors to the lone courtroom. They took their seats in the second pew, and waited for the Judge to enter. It didn't take long. The court clerk stood and announced, "All rise, the honorable Judge Henry Stone presiding." When the Judge took his seat, they all sat back down. The docket was fairly light, so they were the third case to be called. The deputy escorted the Compton's to the defendant's table, and Carla followed them. She identified herself to the Judge, and informed him that she was Canadian, and was indeed, licenced to practice in Washington State. After the Compton's stated their full names, dates of birth and address, the clerk read the charges, and the Judge asked the defendants it they understood them. They both replied, "yes." The prosecutor then went into detail of the government's case. "The defendants were arrested at the Friday Harbor U.S. customs shed, after a search of their sailboat resulted in agents finding marijuana in the keel. Subsequently the contraband was removed, tested and weighed. It resulted in a seizure of fourteen ten-kilogram bags of the drug, for a total of one hundred forty kilograms. Approximately 309 pounds." The Judge asked, "How do you plead." In unison Frank and Margaret replied, "Not guilty." "Bail" the Judge inquired, directing his question to the prosecutor. "As this seizure is of a serious quantity, and the defendants aren't U.S. citizens, the government requests they be remanded until the preliminary hearing." Carla spoke up immediately, "Mr. and Mrs. Compton are seniors with no criminal history. They have property and family in Vancouver, where they have lived all of their lives. The boat was just recently purchased through an R.C.M.P. auction, and they have no idea how the drugs got there. They are not a risk for flight, and are just as anxious to clear this up as the court is." Judge Stone replied, "I agree with the prosecution, this seizure is of a very serious quantity, however, with no prior criminal record, and well established roots to their community, I'm reluctant to remand. Bail is set at one-hundred-thousand dollars, cash or bond. Preliminary hearing is set fifteen days from today, at the U.S. District Court in Seattle." Carla told the Compton's to be patient, that she would contact Steven, as soon as they left the courtroom, so he could start making bail arrangements. She would have them home by tomorrow afternoon.

CHAPTER FOUR

Jake and Carla walked out of the court, into a sunny, warm June afternoon. "Before we call Steven", Jake said, "We have two options. We can head back to the airport and home for the night, just to return tomorrow, to bail them out, or, have you ever been to Roche Harbor?" "No," she responded. I've been to several of the Gulf Islands but never the San Juan's." "It's an old lime quarry town, over a hundred twenty-five years old. The quarry is long gone, but the town was converted into a resort, with all kinds of character. I think you'll like it." She knew what an over night meant, and it didn't take her long to accept the offer. "I'll call my office and have my assistant juggle my calendar....again. I'll give Steven a call as well, and get him to transfer the bail money into my trust account today, so I'll see it by tomorrow."

Jake called a taxi, and they drove the ten miles to Roche Harbor.   As they pulled into the resort, Carla knew she was going to like this.   The white, colonial, Hotel de Haro, stood out amidst the lush, green landscaping, as it sat proudly surveying the three hundred seventy-seven-slip marina.   Carla followed Jake to the office as he registered them. The front desk clerk handed them the keys to a second floor room, overlooking the grounds, and marina.   The romantic setting wasn't lost on either of them.

It was getting close to dinnertime, so they both showered and headed down to McMillin's Bistro.   The hostess seated them, and handed them menus. Jake looked at his watch, and saw it was seven twenty five. He looked over at Carla and told her, "Sunset is around nine fifteen this time of year.   That should give us plenty of time to finish a leisurely dinner, and head over to Madrona for drinks, and the best sunset this side of Key West. She responded with "are you trying to seduce me" which she followed up with an alluring grin.   They both laughed out loud. When the waitress came over, Jake ordered the Spring Wild Mushroom Basket to share, and the Bronzed Alaskan Wild King Salmon for himself. Carla ordered the Parmesan Crusted Petrale Sole. Jake knew now, that he didn't have to fly tonight, so they decided to share a bottle of Pinot Noir with dinner. While they waited for their food, Carla became serious. "I hate to ruin the mood, but we need to discuss the case. On the surface, the government looks to have a pretty solid case. Short of some kind of procedural error, or irregularities in the chain of custody with the evidence, it comes down to Frank and Margaret's word, which isn't much of a defense. With a street value of over a million U.S. dollars, they could be looking at up to twenty years. We have to move forward assuming the other side, has crossed all their T's and dotted their I's. That drops it back into your lap. When we get back to the mainland, you'll need to track down the history of this sailboat. Who owned it, how it came into the hands of the R.C.M.P., the timelines, etcetera." Jake agreed, "It doesn't seem fair. So much for innocent until proven guilty. Proving them innocent *before* it gets to trial is our best bet." "Yes, maybe our only bet" she replied. Their meals came and they enjoyed them with no more talk about business. By the time they finished eating and quaffed down the last of the Pinot it was nearing nine. This time Carla took care of the check and they walked the few paces down to Madrona.

Madrona was another colonial style building, with an almost New Orleans vibe to it. It extended out over the water, and if you were on the deck when the tide was in, you could see the water, through the deck boards. The sun was already low in the sky, when they grabbed a table for two, outside along the rail. Jake ordered a couple of Brandies for them, and waited for the sun to set. Carla let out a sigh. "It was every bit as spectacular, as you said it would be." They finished their drinks and walked hand in hand back to their room.

As soon as they closed and locked the door, he pulled her close, their lips found each other, and they held the embrace for long time. When they did finally separate, they couldn't undress fast enough. They had barely gotten into bed when Jake's cell phone went off. "Jake here" he answered. "Jake, it's Steven. On top of everything else that's happening, I just got to my parent's house to check on things, and it looks like they've had a break in." "Have you called the police?" "They're on their way." "Ok, don't touch anything until they get there, and call me back when they leave." "Alright, I'll talk to you shortly." Carla could tell what had happened, having heard Jake's end of the conversation. The mood was gone…for now. They flipped on the television and sat up in bed waiting for Steven's call.

It was about forty-five minutes later when Steven called again. "Well, what's the damage?" Jake asked. "It's strange. The place was ransacked, but nothing appears to be stolen. Mom and Dad will have to do an inventory when they get home, but for now it looks ok." "Good," Jake replied, "not much more we can do tonight, lock it up and we'll see you tomorrow. Oh, by the way, any problems with the money transfer to Carla's account?" "No, it's all good, talk to you tomorrow." Jake turned out the light, pulled Carla close, and uttered, "Now where were we?"

CHAPTER FIVE

Jake woke to an overcast sky, but it was forecast to burn off, so the flight home would be no problem. Carla was still asleep, as he lay next to her, just watching her breathe. He cherished the brief moments they spent together, and never took them for granted. When she stirred a little, he moved closer to spoon her. Carla felt his warm body against hers. She rolled over to face him, and whispered, "good morning." Her hand traced his body, until she found what she was looking for.

When they were both satisfied, and exhausted, they showered, together this time, dressed and went down to the office to check out. Jake asked the clerk to call them a taxi, and they walked next door to the Lime Kiln Café. By the time they were finished their toast and coffee, the taxi had arrived.

The twenty-minute drive back to town, got them to the Wells Fargo Bank, shortly after ten. Carla went into the bank to make the money transfer arrangements, and after Jake paid the driver he joined her. When they had finished, they walked to the courthouse, and did the paperwork with the clerk. "It'll take a couple of hours for it go through," Carla reported, "want to go for a walk?" "Sure." Like most harbor towns, Friday Harbor was built on a hill, sloping down to the water. The view was impressive. As they walked down First Street, Carla noticed a hanging wooden sign, "The Bean Café." "Cappuccinos?" she offered, "my treat." "You had me at cappuccino." They got their drinks to go. and continued down to the marina. They both loved boats. Jake had only sailed a few times on friend's boats, but Carla on the other hand, was quite an accomplished sailor. She and her husband owned a thirteen-meter Jeanneau, which they had sailed as far south as Ensenada. They walked the floats for the next hour or so just kicking keels. Carla looked at her watch and said, "let's go rescue the Compton's."

When they arrived back at the courthouse, the paperwork was complete. The two of them walked across the street to the Sheriff's office and picked up their clients. A quick taxi ride back to the airport, and they were finally on their way home. During the flight, Jake and Carla brought them up to speed, about the break in.

When the Cessna touched down again at Boundary Bay, they cleared Customs, and Steven was there to meet them. "Welcome back!" he greeted them. Let's get you home."

When they pulled up in front of their house in North Vancouver, everything looked normal from the outside. As they walked through the front door, they could see, the same didn't apply to the interior. Steven jumped in, "sorry, but I thought it best not to touch anything. This way you can see what was disturbed, and see if anything is missing. As they moved from room to room, reorganizing as they went, nothing seemed to be missing. When they got to the desk in Frank's den, Frank noticed, he couldn't find the lease agreement with the marina, for his boat slip. It didn't make any sense. Why would anyone be interested in that? When they had gone through the entire house they agreed, it was enough for one day. When

Steven left, he called Jake with the update. Jake figured the marina would be as good a place to start as any, and told him, to have him and his father, meet him at the marina, at nine o'clock tomorrow morning.

The next morning Jake was up early, and on the road. He knew bridge traffic would be a zoo. He thought to himself, how he enjoyed the laid back pace of island life, as brief as it was. When he got off the Lion's Gate bridge, he stayed on ninety-nine to exit four. From there he snaked his way along Westport Road, down the hill until it met Marine Drive, which took him the rest of the way to the marina. He was a few minutes early, so he sat in his car, in the parking lot, and waited for Steven and Frank. In about ten minutes, the two men pulled into the parking space beside him. Jake noticed that another car, a dark blue Chevy Malibu, seemed to follow them in, and parked at the far end of the parking lot, next to the main road. He didn't give it too much attention, as this was a popular marina, with a lot of people coming and going.

The three of them got out of their vehicles and exchanged   greetings,   then headed over to the marina office. "Good morning Jimmy," Frank said to the marina manager, who stood up from his desk, to shake his hand. "Good morning to you too" he replied. "Jimmy, this is my son Steven and our friend Jake." "Nice to meet you" he said, as he reached out to shake their hands. "I though you were away for week." "Long story" Frank replied, I'll tell you over a coffee sometime." "Look Jimmy, my house got ransacked yesterday sometime, and the only thing that I can see missing is my copy of the slip lease agreement. Who the hell would be interested in that?" "No problem," Jimmy replied, "I can run you off another copy right now." "That'd be great, but what I really wanted to ask, was if you noticed anyone checking out my slip, or asking questions?" "Ya, come to think of it, there was a guy came in yesterday, just as I was closing up. He asked if I knew where the boat was headed. I told him no. He thanked me and left. I finished locking up, and headed out right away. Didn't give it another thought, until just now." Jake took over, "do you recall what the guy looked like?" "Sure, maybe six foot tall, two-twenty, two-thirty, bald, looked like he worked out." "Age?" "Thirtyish." "Did you notice anything distinguishing about him?" "He had a tattoo, I think it was a lightning bolt, on the right side of his neck. Not your typical yachtie look." "That's a great help," Jake said, thanking him for his time.

When they left the office, Jake noticed the Blue Malibu was still parked in the far corner of the lot, driver behind the wheel. He told Steven not to drive away until he signaled them. He then went to the trunk of his car and pulled out a medium sized leather duffle, and got back into the driver's seat. Unzipping the duffle, he pulled out a digital camera, with a five hundred millimeter telephoto lens. Zooming the lens in, he snapped off a half dozen shots, of the car's licence plate, and it's driver. He then motioned for Steven and Frank to leave, while he stayed back to observe. When they turned right, onto Marine Drive, the Malibu fell in behind them, about a block back. Jake fell in behind the Malibu, about two blocks back. Between the curves and the hills, a loose tail was almost impossible. Jake tried to close the gap but was having trouble making up time in traffic. The blue Malibu was having the same problem. Somewhere around Fifteenth Street he got trapped at a traffic light. It didn't matter, he knew where Frank lived. By the time Jake was nearing the north end of the Lion's Gate, he too was following a ghost.

Jake got off at the south end of the bridge, and headed straight for his office. He pulled the SD card from his camera, and loaded it into the slot in his computer. The photos loaded immediately, and were crystal clear. When he blew them up to full screen he got what he wanted, a perfect shot of the licence plate, and a clean shot of the driver. When he saw that the shot of the driver, matched the marina managers description of the mystery visitor, Jake new he had his first solid lead.

From his other job, he had made numerous contacts with both the Vancouver police and R.C.M.P. Getting an ID to go along with the plate number, should be a breeze. He opened up his contact app, and brought up the name Rick Boiko. He called Rick on his personal cell, and got an answer after a couple of rings. "Rick, Jake Walker here." "Jake, how are you, it's been a while?" "Sure has. I don't know if you're aware, but I left the tech firm a while back, and branched out on my own." "Congratulations, how's it going?" "Pretty mundane, until a couple of days ago, but it's starting to get interesting, that's why I'm calling." "Sure, what can I do for you?" Rick asked. "Can you run a plate for me?" "Should I ask what it's about?" "No, best to stay arms length for now. I'll catch you up if anything pans out." "Ok go ahead, I'll see what I can do. I'm just on the way to the station, I'll have to get back to you." Jake gave him the number and said good-bye.

He picked up the phone and dialed Carla. When she answered, he asked where she was with the legal side of things. "Do you feel like a return trip to San Juan Island?" "Yes," he replied, "but don't you think we should stay focused on the case?" "I'm talking about the case, but glad to know you're thinking about me." "What's up?" "I'd like to take a first hand look at that boat. I'm not sure what I expect to find, but it's a place to start. Could we go this afternoon, we'd be back by dark?" "That works for me. You had lunch?" "Just finished." "Ok, let me grab a quick sandwich and I'll pick you up at your office." "Great, just pull up front. I'll watch for you." That worked out well for Jake. Carla's office was a storefront on Hornby, just up from Robson. Parking would be tough this time of day. As promised, she was waiting when he arrived.

CHAPTER SIX

They were in the air and headed south by two o'clock, and in a taxi to the marina by two forty-five. The boat had been hauled out of the water, and was sitting on bunks, in a fenced yard at the marina. When Carla contacted the prosecutor to get discovery information, he said they had finished with the boat, and it was now being held for possible forfeiture, pending the disposition of the file. He had no problem with the defense examining it.

They found the marina manager, who escorted them to the boat, and found them a ladder, so they could climb up to inspect the interior. A quick external inspection, showed the keel had been removed and was blocked up, unattached to the hull. When they entered the cabin, they observed that the cabin sole had been pulled up, and they could see the ground through the keel holes in the bilge. Carla indicated that she couldn't see anything that would help the case, so they climbed back down the ladder, for a closer look at the keel. When Jake accidentally leaned against it, he was startled when it actually wobbled. "Well that's strange," he offered. Carla agreed. "A keel for a boat this size should weigh in at four thousand pounds or more. It shouldn't have budged." Jake looked in through the top, and could see it was hollow. This was no surprise, it was where the drugs were found. What was a surprise, was that when the two of them tried to move it again, it moved quite easily. When they went to try and lift it, it felt extremely light for a keel, maybe a couple of hundred pounds. As they took an even closer look, they could see that it was nothing more than a fiberglass shell. Instead of more than four thousand pounds of lead ballast, the keel consisted of about five hundred pounds of fiberglass and pot. The color drained from Carla's face. She looked at Jake and said, "It's a good thing they weren't trying to sail in a stiff breeze. There wasn't enough ballast to keep the boat upright, and they would have been in a worse predicament than they're in now." "Jake added, "This was well planned out, and didn't just happen overnight. The Compton's said that they purchased the boat about six weeks ago. We need to find out the time line, from when they took delivery, until it went into the water. I'll contact them as soon as we get back. Are we done here?" " Let me get a few photos and we're out of here." When she was done they thanked the manager, and headed back toward the marina office.

As they were walking, Jakes cell went off. "Jake here." "Hey, it's Rick, can you talk?" "Sure" Jake replied, "go ahead." "Are you tracking the elderly these days?" he asked. "No, what are you talking about?" "The plate number you gave me, tracks back to a two-thousand and twelve Honda Accord, owned by a seventy-two year old widow." Jake responded, "The car I saw it on, was a late model Chevrolet Malibu, and that was no widow, behind the wheel. Is it possible the plate was stolen and she doesn't even know it yet?" "Sure, it happens all the time. We'll follow up with her, on our end. Sorry I wasn't of much help." "I appreciate your help. I owe you one." Carla had a confused look on her face. Jake relayed to events of the morning to Carla. She asked, "Should I be concerned?" "No more than usual. As a criminal lawyer, you know as well as I do, where there's drugs, there's the potential for danger." "Yes, that is very true." They found a taxi by the marina office, and returned to the plane.

When they landed back on the mainland, Jake dropped Carla back at her office, and continued on to his. The first call he made was to Frank. Frank was surprised to find out that they had been followed. Jake advised him to just go about his normal day-to-day business, but to stay aware of his surroundings, as well as, any strangers, or strange activity. If he noticed anything out of the ordinary, he was instructed to call Jake immediately. "Before you hang up," Jake added, "Without being obvious, are you able to look out a window, and see if there are any vehicles that you don't recognize from the neighborhood?" "I can't see the street. The yard is surrounded by a six foot cedar hedge." "Don't worry about it then. Just take a look, any time you coming or going." Jake couldn't help but think, "Hedges and fences, great privacy, but unless they're topped with razor wire, lousy security."

The next call he made was to his old school buddy, Sgt. Peter McDaniel at the

Burnaby R.C.M.P. detachment. They had both graduated from the Police Studies Undergraduate Program, at Simon Fraser University. Peter went on to pursue a career with the Mounties, while Jake went for a more lucrative path in the private sector. "Pete" Jake said when Peter answered, "How's my favorite Queen's Cowboy?" It was a term Peter didn't really care for, but he tolerated it, because of whom it was coming from. "I'm doing great" he replied, "Are you still whoring yourself out to the Corporate world?" Jake chuckled, "No, as a matter of fact I just recently moved to private practice." "How's that going so far?" Peter asked. "A little soft until a few days ago, until a big one dropped into my lap. That's why I'm calling, I need your help." "What can I do?" Jake brought him up to date about the boat, the dope and the arrest. He left out the part about the stranger in the car, for now. He told Peter, "I need to know the history of the boat, prior to it being sold at auction. How you guys got involved, who was the previous owner, etc." "Alright, I'll need the name of the buyer, boat registration, the auction, and date he purchased it." "No problem, I'll fire you off an email as soon as I get it. And thanks." They hung up, and Jake leaned back in his chair, took a deep breath, and wondered to himself, what his next step would be. He had decided, it would be dinner, a drink and then early to bed. He would get the information he need, first thing in the morning.

CHAPTER SEVEN

The next morning rolled in, along with the clouds, wind and rain. Jake showered, dressed, grabbed his umbrella and was on his way to the office by eight o'clock. He parked his car, and stopped in at Starbuck's, to grab a bagel and a dark roast to go. His first priority, was to call the Compton's. Margaret answered, "Good morning Mr. Walker, if you're looking for Frank, he just went out for his morning walk." "Please, just call me Jake. You may even be able to help me." He told her. Jake went on to explain to her what information he needed. She responded. "I think I know where he filed that stuff, just hold for a minute." A couple of minutes later Margaret returned to the phone. "I found it," and she proceeded to relay the information he needed, which he immediately fired off, in an email to Peter. He had barely hit the send key, when his phone rang. It was Margaret, and she sounded barely coherent. "Frank just called, and he said some men have him, and won't release him, until he returns the merchandise he stole, what are they talking about?" Jake knew right away what they were talking about. He replied, "I think they may be talking about the drugs in your boat." "But we don't have them, you know that." "I do, but they don't, and probably won't believe him anyhow." "Frank also said, if we involve the police they know where Steven and his family live, and would hurt them. I don't know what I'm supposed to do." Jake thought for a minute then told her, "At some point we have to get the police involved, but for now, leave it with me. Have you called Steven?" "Not yet" She replied. "Ok, let me call him and explain the situation." She agreed and they hung up.

He dialed Steven's number. It was answered after a couple of rings. Jake briefed Steven, and told him to take his family, and go to his parents place, and stay there. He agreed, and said he would be there within the hour. Jake called Carla, and brought her up to speed. She said, "I don't agree with not bringing the police in." "I need to find out what we're dealing with here. If it's just a couple of local dealers, I have all the confidence in the world that the police can protect the family, but if it's bigger than that, we don't know what kind of reach these guys have. We also have to find a safe house for the family, do you know of any place?" "I have a condo at Whistler that would work." "Great, pick them up and take them there. Don't forget to forward their phone to the condo. When you get back into the city, call me." There wasn't much more Jake could do until he heard back from Pete.

During the two-hour drive to Whistler, Carla got to know the Compton's on a personal level. Steven was a marketing manager for a local shipping firm. His wife was a stay at home mom for his two young girls. Frank was a retired accountant, who had had a private practice on the north shore, while Margaret had a full time career, volunteering in the community.

Jake was getting impatient. He picked up the phone, and called Pete. Peter answered right away. "Good morning Jake" he said. "Your timing couldn't have been any better, I just got the file, in my email. Here's the scoop. "Your client purchased the boat, May second of this year. Prior to that, it was a proceeds of crime seizure related to a drug conviction. The person it was taken from was a Lyle Kohler, who's doing two and a half years in Kent Institution, near Agassiz, for cultivation, and distribution of marijuana." "Where was this guy from?" Jake asked. "I can't really go into detail, but if you were to start looking in the area between Kaslo and New Denver, you might get lucky. FYI, Lyle had a brother, Leonard. Off the record, we suspect he is involved, but don't have enough evidence to move forward." "Thanks Pete," Jake said, his IOU list, getting longer by the day. "One more thing," Pete added. "These are nasty guys. The growers up that way, are extremely protective of their crops. If you do go sniffing around, and come up with anything, I'd appreciate a call." "I promise, you'll be the first."

Jake dialed Carla. "Where are you?" he asked. Just passed Squamish, on my way back to the city." "Are you up for a road trip? It may be for a couple of days." "Sure, I

need to pack an overnight bag. Can you pick me up at my place in a couple of hours?" "See you soon then." He agreed.
40

He got to Carla's right on time. They decided to take her car, as his would stick out like a neon light, in that part of the country, at least more so than her twenty-fourteen Acura. Jake had a lot to catch her up on.

CHAPTER EIGHT

By the time they reached Vernon, it was ten o'clock. They wouldn't make the last ferry at Needles, crossing Arrow Lake, so they decided to grab a room. The only one they could find still showing a vacancy, was the Pacific Inn and Suites on Hwy. 97, at the north end of town. It would do. They were both exhausted, so Jake set his alarm for five the next morning, and they were both asleep within minutes.

When the alarm went off, Jake awoke to Carla snuggled next to him. She whispered, "this is nice, can't we just lay here for an hour….or two?" As much as it pained Jake to say no, they had another four-hour drive, and a full day ahead of them. After a quick bite of toast and coffee in lobby breakfast nook, they hit the road.

Shortly after nine, Jake's phone rang, it was Steven's number on the call display. "What's up?" he answered. "I just got another call from Dad. He says he's alright but they either want their drugs, or five hundred thousand dollars." "Have they given a time line?" "No, he said he would call back later. I have access and signing authority for his investment account, so I can arrange for the money." "Fine, start working on that, but don't agree to turn it over until you talk to me." Steven agreed and they hung up.

For the next hour or so, neither of them spoke much. The wet weather they left back on the coast, seemed to follow them eastward. The heavy rain, turn to a light steady drizzle, low clouds smothering the mountaintops. It had an almost hypnotizing effect. Jake was deep in thought, he wasn't even certain what his game plan was going to be when they got there. As his mind drifted, his thoughts traced back to many years ago, when he had his Harley Road King. This would be a great touring road, in the right weather. Lots of curves, little traffic. Jake remembered one of his favorite pleasures about riding, was the smells he took in as he rode. The smell of farmland, the spruce and pine forests. It was a huge contrast, to the smells of car exhaust, and back alley dumpsters, that the city had to offer. He had given up riding soon after graduating and starting his career. He just didn't have the time. Maybe when he slows down a bit, and starts to put himself first, he'll ride again.

Carla spoke, and Jake was back in the present. "Why don't we review what we have so far?" She said. Jake agreed. She started, "Here's what I have to date;" "First, the Compton's purchased the boat from a police auction in May, they took immediate delivery, and took it directly to the marina. Then, according to Frank, it sat on the trailer for just two days, before the marina staff craned it into the water. It would be impossible to fabricate a fiberglass keel, and install it in two days, never mind without any of the marina staff noticing. Once in the water it would also be impossible. Next, it sat in the water, for five more weeks. Again, no opportunity, to install the fake keel. Then, the Compton's are arrested attempting to enter the United States. Next thing, someone   ransacks   their house, while they are in a Washington jail. After that, they're followed when they leave the marina. Then the big one, Frank gets kidnapped near his home. Shortly after, the family receives the first of two ransom calls from Frank. And finally, the second ransom call. Does that sound about right?" "It does." Jake agreed.   Carla also added, that she spoke to the federal prosecutor, and asked him, if the R.C.M.P. backed up Frank and Margaret's story about the boat sale, would they drop the charges? He said he wouldn't, he doesn't contest how they acquired the boat, the fact is, that they had six weeks to hide the contraband. "So nothing has changed. Our only hope is to find the person, or persons, who actually did it." She summed up.

About an hour later they pulled up to the west side terminus of the Needles ferry. It had just left, and it would be about a half hour before it got back. They were starting to crave coffee but knew there wouldn't be much before Nakusp, and that wouldn't be for another hour or so.   With it being a short sleep the night before, the two of them reclined the seats for a quick power nap.

As she closed her eyes, Carla flashed back to her earlier years, and the path that got her here today. She grew up in Kamloops, and earned her law degree at Thompson Rivers University there. After graduation, she moved to Vancouver, and articled at a mid sized firm, where she specialized in criminal law. As much as she loved to practice, she didn't like the rat race environment, firms of that size fostered. After a couple of years, she decided to go it on her own. The hours weren't any better, but they were her hours, and she didn't have to compete for her position in the corporate pecking order. It was about that time, when she met her husband to be. He was a commodities broker. They were both committed to their careers, which ultimately led to the failure of their marriage. The breakup was amicable. They were both to blame. She was also getting to the point in her life, where she wanted to slow down a bit, and smell the proverbial roses.

They were jolted back to consciousness, by the blast of the horn, from the arriving ferry. Soon they were on board the single deck vessel, along with about half a dozen other vehicles. When they docked on the east side of the lake, they continued the drive north to

Nakusp. They spotted Chumley's Restaurant, and thought it looked interesting enough. When they got inside they found a table, and both ordered the fish and chips. That would hold them until dinnertime. When they finished, they ordered a couple of coffees to go, for the short forty-minute drive to New Denver.

When they arrived at New Denver, Jake decided the best plan, was to check in with the local R.C.M.P. detachment, and see what light they could shine on the Kohler brothers. A lone member was seated at a desk, talking on the phone. He hung up, and asked what he could help them with. Jake explained who they were, and what they were looking for. The member replied, "I've been expecting you. Sgt. McDaniel called and gave us a heads up you may be coming." Carla responded with, "Wasn't that considerate of him," as she looked at Jake. "Yes, it was," he answered back, all the while knowing the real reason, was so the members could keep tabs on them. "What can you tell us about the Kohlers?" Jake asked. "Well, they've been here all their lives. Built a reputation as the county bullies, a reputation well deserved. They have a small farm, a bit less than half way between here and Kaslo. You already know about Lyle. We're pretty sure Leonard's just as guilty, but Lyle took the rap, and we didn't have enough on Leonard to charge him." "Where was their grow op?" "In the mountains, about three kilometers south of their place. It's since been eradicated." "Did you ever notice a sailboat?" "Sure, when we raided the property, there was a thirty footer in the barn. That's the one that was sold at auction." "Was it ever searched for drugs?" Jake continued. "Yes, the entire property was searched, both by members and drug dogs. There was marijuana everywhere, the dogs would have alerted to a general area, then at that point, they would nave been removed, and it would become a manual search. We visually searched the boat, but if there was no indication of tampering, we wouldn't have taken it apart." "Well, U.S. Customs found the drugs in the keel, and there wasn't enough time for our clients to put it there, so we suspect that they were there the entire time. When was the last time you saw Leonard?" "A couple of weeks ago, but that's not unusual, he's not what you would call, "the social type"" the Mountie answered. "When he does hang out, it's with a pretty rough crowd. Mostly biker types. No gang affiliations that we're aware of. They have some survivalist buddies from Idaho, but nothing to indicate ties to white supremacists, or any other radical groups." "Well ok, thanks for all your help. I think we'll poke around in town a bit, if it's ok with you guys, and then head back." "Good luck, and be careful. You'll get squat from his pals, and the rest of the folks, are too afraid to say anything against the Kohler boys. If you run into any trouble, give us a call." "Again thanks."

Jake and Carla left the detachment and got into their car. "Let's try the local coffee shop, they usually know everyone in town." Carla suggested. "Great idea, I'll buy," he answered. They started driving around, until they spied a sign saying "Apple Tree Sandwich Shop" hanging from an old converted house, next to the Home Hardware store. They looked at each other, grinned and nodded in agreement. As they walked through the door, a woman who looked to be in her mid sixties greeted them, with friendly "hello." Jake spoke, "two coffees, and what do you recommend to go with them?" "How about a couple of fresh cinnamon buns?" she asked, "They're still warm from the oven. If you want to take a table, I'll bring them right out." They found a small table for two, by the window overlooking the street. The lady was right behind them with their coffee and pastries. Jake poured it on a little, "Wow, these are the best cinnamon buns I've had in years. You make em?" "I sure did, glad you like them." She answered with an air of pride in her voice. "Hey," he added, "Do you know a Leonard Kohler from these parts?" Her tone changed, "Ya, haven't seen him, don't know where he is," as she walked away indicating in no uncertain terms, that this conversation was over. When they had finished their coffees, Jake left a twenty on the counter by the cash register as they left. Carla spoke, "I don't think this is time well spent." "Agreed," he replied. "Let's see if we can find their place." Carla responded with a surprised, "Then what?" "Don't know, I'll figure that out when we get there." Carla just rolled her eyes, this went against everything she had been taught in law school.

They drove towards Kaslo. After about twenty minutes, they saw a beat up gray, metal mailbox on a post, with the name Kohler, in faded red letters. "This looks like the place." Jake declared. He turned into the drive. The house was about a hundred yards back from the road. It was well hidden, by a row of spruce and pine trees, along the roadside.   As they drove slowly toward the house, they scanned the yard. It was difficult to see anything much past the main house. The rain over the past few days had saturated the air, and a heavy mist, hung over the property, presenting an eerie, surreal atmosphere. To the left of the house, was large barn, with what looked like, a storage shed next to it. When they stopped, Jake got out, while Carla stayed in the car. He approached the house and knocked on the door. After waiting a reasonable length of time, he motioned for Carla to join him. They both felt uneasy, for no apparent reason. There didn't seem to be any sign of life, so they decided to take a look around the property. As they rounded the side of the house, they noticed a crude lane, snaking its way in the opposite direction from the road. After a couple of hundred yards, a clearing appeared out of the mist. The vegetation had been trampled and packed, as though this place was a makeshift parking lot. There were several paths leading away from the clearing. Carla spoke up, "This has "Deliverance" written all over it, let's get outta here." "Just a quick look." Jake said, in a reassuring voice, "besides, help is only a phone call away," as he looked at his cell phone, he could see there was no signal. "Or perhaps not," he added. As they moved slowly, further and further along the path, and into the forest, the mid afternoon sun, sent rays, angling down through the tops of the tall trees. They soon spotted what looked to be targets of some sort. When they got closer, they could see what looked like a shooting range, for both bows and guns. Some targets were nailed to trees, others were free standing. The only time Jake had seen anything like this, was on an assault range. He finally said, "That's enough out here, let's head back.

While they retraced their steps, Jake and Carla were torn, between the beauty and serenity, and the straight up eeriness, that surrounded them. When they neared the main yard they headed toward the barn. The large sliding doors where open about three feet. Jake carefully poked his head in, and let his eyes adjust. There were no lights on, but the sunlight filtering in, between the dried, shrunken boards that sided the barn, was all that was needed. They accentuated the dust particles hanging in the air amidst the humidity. It appeared empty so they continued inside. The two of them stood just inside the doorway and surveyed the interior. Nothing seemed out of the ordinary, for a barn. In the far corner they saw a blue, rip stop tarp, covering something, so they eased their way over to it. Suddenly, something caught the corner of Carla's eye and she let out a scream. Jake turned, just in time to see a large, black and tan dog, charging toward them. He grabbed Carla by the arm, and pulled her in behind him. At about five feet away, the dog lunged. He stopped suddenly, yelped and dropped to the ground, as his hind end overtook his head and shoulders. He had reached the end of the fifty-foot chain, that had him tethered to the backside of the barn. "Jesus Christ!" Jake yelled, as he bent over to catch his breath. "That scared the hell out of me. Are you ok?" "Yes, but I may have a bit of a bruise on my arm." She said, still shaking. "I'll kiss it better later." He replied laughing. By now the dog was back up on his feet, straining on his chain, to get at them. His piercing bark, and teeth glistening with saliva, made the pair, more than a little unsettled. "I think the tarp is out of the dogs range, let's keep going." When they got there, Jake pulled the tarp back. Under it was a roll of fiberglass, along with a couple of half filled, five-gallon plastic pails. One said resin, and the other gel coat. There was also a one-gallon pail, labeled hardener. Jake took a couple of photos with his cell phone, before they replaced the tarp, and continued looking around the barn. They were hoping to find a sailboat keel, or something else, that could have been used for a mold. After a few more minutes of searching around, out of the dogs reach, they found nothing else of interest, so they headed back toward the door. As they emerged, they were greeted by mountain of man. Six three, looked to be about three hundred pounds, with greasy, shoulder length hair, and tattoo sleeves, up and down both arms. The man had a shotgun in his right hand. "Who the fuck are you, and what are you doing here?" Jake uttered nervously, "My name is Jake and we're just looking for the owner." "What do want with him." The stranger asked. "I'm a realtor from Vancouver, and I'm looking for property up this way for a client," Jake answered, hoping the man wouldn't ask for a business card. "Well, he ain't here, and you ain't got no business being here neither." he said. "Now get lost. If I see you around here again, I'll use this." He added, waving the gun. Jake and Carla weren't about to argue. They got into the car and sped out onto the highway and back to New Denver. "I think we need to quit, while we still have our skin in tact." Carla offered. Jake answered, "I'll second that, councilor."

Neither spoke a word, all the way back to New Denver. By the time they arrived, their heart rates were back to normal. "It's been a long day," Carla said, "why don't we just grab a room here and head out in the morning." "I was thinking the same thing," Jake answered. They found a motel just off the highway, that had a pub attached to it. It wasn't much, but it at least appeared clean. After they had checked in, they wandered over to the pub, and ordered beer and burgers. After their last experience in town, they decided not to ask any questions. When they finished eating, they returned to their room, and turned on the television. Lying beside one another, felt so natural. Soon they were in each other's arms, and made love, as if it was their last day on earth.

By next morning, the rain had stopped, and the clouds were starting to break up. They showered, dressed, and went out to put their bags in the car. As they opened the door to their room, they could see that someone had paid them a visit in the night. Across the windshield, some moron had spray painted, "GO HOME", in black paint. They knew reporting it to the police would be pointless. Jake remembered the Home Hardware next to the café they were at yesterday, so he walked over, and got a couple of razor blades. They spent the next hour scraping the paint off the windshield. At least it was good enough to get them home. Jake and Carla had both had enough of this place, so they decided to drive to Nakusp for breakfast.

While they were eating, Jakes phone rang. It was Rick Boiko with the Vancouver police department. "Jake, I finally got a hit on that photo of the driver you sent me a few days ago. His name is Leonard Kohler. His last known address is New Denver. And Jake," he added, he's not a nice guy. If you have any beef with him, it's best you come to me." "Alright," Jake replied, "I'm just out of town right now, and will contact you when I get back. Thanks." There was so much Jake wanted to tell his buddy, but he wasn't ready yet. Soon, he thought.

It was around dinnertime, when Jake dropped Carla at her place, then went directly to his office. He called Steven with an update, on what he and Carla had found out. Steven told him, there was no more communication from Frank, and they were getting more and more worried, by the minute. "I think it's about time we had a meeting with everyone present" Jake suggested. "How about Carla and I come up to Whistler in the morning, around eleven?" "Sounds good" Steven replied. "We'll have coffee and lunch ready when you get here." Jake called Carla and updated her.

CHAPTER NINE

The drive up to Whistler was uneventful, something they were both appreciative of. When they got to Carla's condo, the family was waiting for them with lunch and coffee, just as promised. Her unit was one of fifty, climbing their way up the side of the slope just north of the village. It was a three bedroom, two story, built in the typical alpine style. In the wintertime she could ski right to her front door.

After a few pleasantries over lunch, it was time to get down to business. Jake said, "I think it's time to bring in law enforcement. Based on what Carla and I have been able to find out so far, we don't believe, who ever it is that has Frank, is part of an organized group. We think it's just one or two individuals, and the rest of you aren't in much danger. Having said that, the condo's not being used anyway, so you might as well stay here for now. As for getting the police involved, we've seen first hand, the type of bad people we are dealing with, and law enforcement can offer resources we just don't have. Another thing, if you have to withdraw that amount of cash from the bank, I'm sure red flags are going to get set off, and the authorities will be poking around anyhow." Carla chimed in, "Let's not forget the fact that if I have to appear in a U.S. Federal Court without Frank. They're going to need to see some sort of police file, or report, to back up the kidnapping." "Carla's right, if it's ok with you, her and I will stay involved, and work with police as much as they will permit us to." Steven spoke up, "We're out of our element here, so we just have to trust your judgment," as he glanced over to his wife and mother. They were nodding in agreement.

"Let's forward your home phone to Steven's cell, and he can return to the city with us. We need him handy to the money, when we have to act." Jake suggested. "Is there anything else the rest of you need for your stay here?" "No," Margaret replied, "I think we're good." "Steven, you can leave your car, and ride with Carla and me. Do you have another vehicle in town?" "Sure, I'll just use my wife's." Before they left, Jake made one more call. "Rick, it's Jake, I think it's time to get you involved in what's happening. It's one o'clock now, can you meet us at my office at four o'clock? I'll explain everything then." He gave Rick the address, and hung up. A quick round of hugs, and they were on their way.

They reached Jake's office right around three thirty. He had just put a pot of coffee on when Rick walked into the room. "Always on time," Jake said to the tall lean man standing in front of him. "Good to see ya," Rick replied. Rick was about six foot one inch, maybe one hundred eighty pounds soaking wet. His hair receded to the midway point on the top of his head, and with the dark thick-rimmed glasses, he looked more like an accountant or actuary, than he did a police detective. The deceiving looks had served him well in many situations. Jake did a quick round of introductions, and they got right down to business. He brought the detective up to date about the boat purchase from the auction, and the time line between then and when it was launched. He went on about the arrest at Friday Harbor, the break in, and finally, the kidnapping. Rick was pissed, "You should have come to me immediately at that point." "I know, I know," Jake replied, "but they seemed to know a lot about the family, and I needed to find out who we were dealing with. Was it one or two individuals, or was it bike or street gangs? From what we have found out so far, it appears to be the former." "Still, you should have come to me. Well, what's done is done, let's move on, and I mean everything on the table." Jake went on the relay the details of their road trip, and what they found out in New Denver. "Ok, let's get moving," Rick said, "law enforcement is already behind. The first thing I will need to do is get a court order for Frank's cell phone logs. I'm guessing Mr. Kohler, is already known to police, so I'll check his jacket and find out about any other family, or known associates. Jake, for now, you and Carla keep yourselves available in case I need you on short notice. Steven, I'm going to assign one of my team to stay with you, should the kidnappers call. He'll be setting up your phone so we can record any calls. Does anybody have any questions? No, okay, I'll talk to you all later." With that, Rick left with Steven, leaving Jake and Carla in the office. "I'm hungry and there's not much we can do for now. How about some dinner?" "Absolutely," Carla replied, "your neighborhood, you pick." "I hope you like Italian."

They walked the block and a half to Al Porto, just off of Water Street, next to the rail yard. It would be easy to miss, if you didn't know where to look. The place was a Gastown staple. It had been there for a few decades, formerly one of Umberto Menghi's. Even though it was under new ownership, the food and the service, lived up to its heritage. It was in the top five for Jake. The hostess sat them at a table in a quiet corner, and left them to look over the menus. Jake knew the menu by heart, so he didn't even pick it up. Carla took a long look. When the waitress returned with their water and drinks, they were ready to order. Jake ordered the Bruschetta to start, and the Spaghettini Pesto Pomodoro, and Carla, the Minestrone and the Veal Piccata. While they ate their meals, the two of them spoke exclusively about their personal lives, no shoptalk. The one thing they had in common, was they both longed to travel, but were so busy with their careers it just never happened for them. Neither of them had taken a real vacation in years. They talked about where they would go, what they would see…when they had the time. "You know, if it's going to happen, we have to make the time. When all this is over, let's get away for a week or two. Somewhere, hot and sunny. What do you say?" Jake asked. "Are you asking me out on a date?" Carla asked with a grin. "I guess I am." They spoke about everything, and nothing, while they finished their meals. When they left the restaurant, Jake invited her to his place for a nightcap. She accepted without hesitation.

The next morning Jake was up early, and Carla awoke to the smell of freshly brewed coffee. As she entered the kitchen, Jake saw that she was wearing nothing but one of his T-shirts, which came down to about mid thigh. "I hope you don't mind?" she asked. "It was all I could find." Jake didn't mind at all, it's the best that T-shirt ever looked. He asked, "are you hungry?" "I am," she replied, "but let me make breakfast, to show you that I'm not just a pretty face." "It'll have to be one hell of a breakfast to top what I'm looking at right now." She blushed a bit and said, "pancakes?" "Sounds great."

They were just clearing the table when Jake's phone rang. It was Rick. "How soon can we meet at your office?" he asked. "We can be there in thirty minutes." Jake replied. "We?" Rick asked, which was quickly followed by a slightly embarrassed, "Oh…Ok see you then." When the two of them arrived at Jake's office, Rick was waiting outside with a tray of Starbuck's coffees. "I took the liberty, must be the cop in me, I hope you don't mind." Jake looked at Carla, "see great instincts, that's what make him such a good cop." They all laughed as Jake unlocked the office and let them in. They took seats, and Jake said, "Ok, what's up." "Quick status report," Rick said. "One of my guys is working on a court order, to get Frank's cell phone records released by his carrier, should have it in a couple of hours. I got my hands on the Kohler brothers records, and found that they have, and I'll us the term loosely" a girlfriend here in town. Her name is Angela Debeau. She's a junky prostitute, with an apartment on East Hastings. Jake I need you come with me, to see her. Carla, I've got nothing for you at the moment." "No problem, I'm playing catch up at my office anyway. Just call me when you need anything." She said goodbye, and walked out the door. Rick turned back to Jake and told him, "the reason I want you there, is to get a good look at her. I don't thinks she's going to give up the brothers, so I need you to brush up on your stakeout skills." "Can you dress down a bit so you can blend in better?" "Sure, I think I can round up some old painting clothes from the condo." They left the office and drove back to Jake's place.

As soon as Jake changed into his "street" clothes Rick drove them to East Hastings, where they found the address listed for Angela. As expected, it was an old dilapidated, brick tenement, six stories high, with an elevator that was out of order. Her apartment was on the fifth floor. Even as they neared the building, they could smell the pungent aroma of body odor and urine, not to mention rotting food. When they did arrive at Angela's door and knocked, it took her a good five minutes to answer it. When she opened it, the two of them saw a woman who looked every bit as someone who belonged there. She stood about five foot four, blonde hair with about an inch of brown root showing. Her eyes were glazed over, and she had the dark, yellow stained fingers, of a chain smoker. She wasn't even trying to hide the needle tracks up and down her arms. Angela looked like a woman in her late forties, but Rick knew from her file, that she was only twenty-seven. They identified themselves, and told her they were looking for Leonard Kohler. "Don't know'im, now fuck off." Was her response. Rick quickly told her, "You're on probation and I think you look stoned. Maybe I should take you in for a drug test. Is that what you want?" "Maybe I do know him, so what." "When was the last time you saw him?" "Not for months." "This is bullshit, get dressed, we're going downtown." Rick told her. "Ok, Ok, I saw him a couple of days ago. He came by, got laid and was out here." "Where does he stay when he's in town?" Rick continued. "Sometimes here, sometimes a hotel downtown, maybe the Kingston." She answered. "Here's my card, call me if you hear from him." "I'll be sure to do that she said, in a not so subtle sarcastic tone." She slammed the door and simultaneously tossed his card into the trash.

Jake and Rick couldn't get out of the building quick enough. Even the urine soaked sidewalk was a breath of fresh air for them. "Alright, this is where you earn your keep." Rick ordered." "Just blend in and keep an eye out for her. If she leaves, try to follow her, but don't, and I repeat, don't, let yourself get into any dangerous situation. Better to lose her, and track her down later, than to scrape you up from some back alley. Call me if anything happens." "Agreed," Jake replied. Rick got in his car and drove toward downtown and the Kingston. After about forty minutes, Jake saw Angela walk out the front door of the building. She had obviously cleaned herself up, as she looked not too bad from a distance. Jake was always amazed at what a woman's makeup could accomplish. He followed her, a block west on the north side of East Hastings, where she stopped at a bus stop. Keeping about half a block behind her, he could see she was waiting for the number sixteen Arbutus bus. When it pulled up to the stop, he quickly caught up and boarded it as well. He knew he was taking a chance on being recognized, but was gambling that her drug haze would prevail. He was right. They continued westbound on Hastings and turned southwest on Howe. Just after Nelson Street, Angela got off through the front door. Jake followed through the rear. He followed her another block down Howe, to the Holiday Inn where she went into the lobby and took a chair. Jake watched from outside. His heart started to race. Stepping off the elevator was the man from the marina, Leonard Kohler. Jake's adrenaline was pumping, and he had to curb his instinct, to rush in and grab him by the throat, demanding to know what the hell was going on. Instead he grabbed his cell phone and called Rick.

Rick had just left the Kingston Hotel when his cell went off. "It's Jake, I found our guy." "Where?" "Shortly after you left, Angela came out, jumped on a bus, and led me here to the Holiday Inn Downtown. They're in the lobby now." "I'm four blocks away. I'll be there in two minutes. If they leave, try to follow them, but don't spook them." They hung up and Jake stayed put. From where he was, Jake could see that Leonard was either angry, or worried. He saw the man give Angela some cash and she got up, walked toward the door and left. Leonard got back onto the elevator. Jake rushed inside to see what floor it stopped at. Seventh, just as Rick entered the lobby.

Jake brought him up to speed, and they both walked over to the front desk. Rick asked to see the manager, and the desk clerk dialed his extension. When the manager approached them, Rick showed his badge, and asked if there was somewhere private they could speak. The manager led them to small office behind the front desk, and asked what this was all about. "We believe a person of interest, in a file we're working, may be staying at this hotel. If you could check your guest registry, we'd appreciate it." "I'm not supposed to release any of our guest information without a warrant." "I know that, but it could be a life or death situation, and we don't have much time. We would really appreciate your cooperation." "Ok, what's the guests name?" "Leonard Kohler." Rick told him. "Nobody by that name registered." He responded, as he turned the computer monitor towards the detective. The men thanked the manager for his cooperation, and went back into the lobby. "He's either just visiting someone, or he's using an alias, and we don't have any known alias's in his file." "Shit!, this was our best lead to date. Can you sit on him for a while?" Rick asked. "You bet. This is so much more fun than chasing paper in the corporate world." Jake replied. "Ya, well don't forget, this is serious, and potentially dangerous. Nobody ever got hurt or killed, by a file folder full of paper." Rick added. "Point taken."

Rick left the hotel, and Jake grabbed a newspaper and a coffee, from the self-serve lobby bar, then took a seat where he could watch the elevators and front entrance. Rick was about half way to police headquarters on Cambie and West Second Avenue when his cell phone started to vibrate. When he answered it was the detective assigned to Steven. "We got another call from Frank." He said. They want the money wire transferred to a numbered account, at the Cayman National Bank." "That's pretty big league, for a couple of Kootenay rednecks like the Kohler brothers, don't you think?" Rick asked. "My thoughts exactly. They're either not as dumb as they appear, or, they have connections that we don't know about." "When do they want the money by?" "Noon tomorrow." The detective answered. "Ok, that doesn't leave us much time then. Once the transfer happens, the money is gone for good. Let's hold off until the last possible minute." "Ten-four." Rick gave Jake a quick call to give him the ransom news, then continued to HQ.

Leonard stepped off the elevator and walked toward the parking garage. Jake put down his newspaper and followed him. As he rounded the corner on the second level of the parkade, he came face to face with Kohler. Leonard grabbed Jake by the throat and pinned him up against the cinder block wall. "Who are you, and why are you following me." He demanded. Jake knew there'd be no bullshitting his way out of this one, so he went with the truth. "I'm looking for a friend who's gone missing, and I think you might know something." He said in a graveled voice, the best he could, while trying to breathe as he spoke. At that point Leonard reached back, and pulled out a military style knife. It was an eight-inch blade with a serrated edge on the top, and a razor sharp smooth one, on the bottom one. The handle was metal, wrapped in braided nylon cord. Rick's words, about the seriousness of this case, flashed back through Jakes brain. "I ain't involved in nothin, so stay out of my business cause next time I'll use this." The bald man warned as he released Jake. When he walked away, Jake was still doubled, over gasping for air. He took a minute to compose himself, then went back into the lobby, and called Rick. Rick said, "Stay put, I'll come and get you. Grab a drink while you're waiting, you've earned it."

By the time Rick arrived, Jake had stopped shaking and was starting to feel like his usual self again. Jake was by no means a guy who was easily intimidated, but he had never been exposed to anything like this, in the corporate security environment, and it caught him off guard. As rick drove them back to the station, he said, "Let's just chalk it up to paying dues. Sometimes the best lessons are the toughest ones." "Amen to that." Was all Jake could think of.

When they got back to the station house, Rick set a pen and pad down in front of Jake, and asked to write a detailed report on the event, while he went off the get them each a cup of coffee. Paperwork, this was something more up Jakes alley. He spent the next forty-five minutes writing his account of the events, and then turned it over to Rick, who read it over, and gave it back to Jake to sign. "Not much more we can do for now," Rick said, "why don't you go clean up, grab something to eat, and I'll call you if anything develops. Where can I drop you?" Jake thought a minute and said, "Carla's office would be great.

When Carla's receptionist called her on the intercom, and whispered over the phone, "There's some homeless looking guy out here to see you. Doesn't have an appointment, but says his name is Jake." When she walked out of her office into reception, her expression went from confused, to polite laughter.

"I'm sorry, you'll have to excuse my laughter, but I've never seen the non GQ side of you before. Come into my office. Wait, do we have to de-louse you first?" she said, still laughing. "Again, I'm sorry, I just couldn't resist." Jake couldn't hold it against her. He realized what he must look like. By the time he relayed the days events to her, she was no longer laughing. "Just let me finish up a couple of things here, and I'll take you home. You can get cleaned up, and I'll take you out for dinner and drinks,…many drinks."

By the time they got to the Bayside Restaurant on English Bay, it was almost seven. When it came to seafood, this was one of Carla's favorites. They got a seat in Kyle's section, and he was on them right away. Kyle was a character. He was flaming, and proud of it, with a personality over the top. He was a part time actor, singer, showman, and would spontaneously launch into popular songs, or show tunes, for his restaurant patrons. Carla always asked for Kyle's section if he was working, and if there was room. When he came to the table, he greeted Carla with hug and a big smile. "And who is this tall hunk of eye candy?" "Kyle, meet Jake, and he's my eye candy, hands off." She responded jokingly. Kyle put forth a pout worthy of an Emmy, followed almost immediately by an ear-to-ear smile. They ordered the Seafood Share Platter and drinks. "You know," she said to Jake, When you told me about your encounter with Leonard, I felt like I was going to be ill. I've never had that kind of a reaction for a man before. I'm afraid of what it may be trying to tell me." He knew exactly how she was feeling. "I don't know how to respond to that." He answered. "Maybe both of us have been in too much control of our lives and careers for so long, it's time to let some things follow their natural paths. Just live for the moment, as they say." "I'd like that very much. It goes against my neatly structured existence, so you'll have to work with me, to learn how to do that." As he looked into her eyes, he reached across the table and gently took both of her hands in his. "That's a project I'm willing to take on."

While Jake and Carla were getting lost in each other, Rick and his squad were working the case. Frank's cell network provider, had forwarded his phone records for the last six months. The detectives were busy pouring over them, looking for call patterns and locations. One thing that did show up, was from the time he was taken, the calls to his home phone, were made from different cell towers around the city. There were also other calls made to numbers Rick was personally tracking down. The general conclusion was, the kidnapper or kidnappers, kept changing locations and for some reason, were using Frank's cell phone for other calls. Again they thought, a bit more complex than they would have expected from the people they were looking at. They would see how far they got tonight, and brief Jake in the morning.

CHAPTER TEN

Jake and Carla awoke from a night of passion, that neither of them believed possible. The newly found emotional element, elevated their physical enjoyment, to a whole new level. They were teenagers again, having just discovered sex for the first time. They liked what they were feeling. Lying awake in each other's arms, they were jolted back to the real world, when Carla's alarm went off. She hopped in the shower while Jake made them a light breakfast of toast, orange juice and coffee. When they finished, Carla drove him home, before she continued on to her office. After showering and a fresh change of clothes, Jake drove to his own office.

His first call was to Rick. "Good morning," Jake said as Rick answered his phone, "tell me you've broken the case." "I'm afraid not yet." He responded, "but we are moving forward. Can you come down to the station?" "I can be there in twenty minutes, can I get you anything on the way?" "No, I'm good, see you shortly." Jake picked up a coffee for himself and box of donuts for the squad room, for a not so subtle attempt for humor. He knew, that at the end of the day, the squad would appreciate them.

When Jake arrived, Rick was on the phone. He waved him over and pointed to a chair in front of his desk. On his way to the desk, he handed the donuts off to a uniformed officer, who thanked him, and took them to the break room. He grabbed a seat in front of Rick's desk, and finished his coffee. "Sorry about that," Rick said, "just got some information back on Mr. Compton's cell phone log. After yesterday our man Leonard is in the wind for sure. The best way to find him again, will be through his contacts. We're pretty sure Angela's phone would be a burner cell, so we have to work backwards and hope we get lucky. Other than the calls from Frank, there's only about a half dozen to other numbers, one of which may be Angela. The one result we do have back so far, is a guy by the name of Charles Hackford, a.k.a. Charlie Crusher or just Crusher. I'm just pulling up his file now." When his record came up on the computer, Rick motioned Jake around to his side of the desk, so he could see the monitor. Jake recognized the photo immediately. "We've met." He went on to relay that part of the New Denver trip to Rick, who responded, "You're lucky, you shouldn't have been on the property in the first place." "This guy has a record for assault, assault with a deadly weapon, threats against a person, numerous drug charges, and that's just his convictions. It doesn't include dropped charges because witnesses were afraid to testify." "Hey, I was just looking for the owner, is that against the law?" "No, but some might see it as trespassing." Rick answered back. "Remember when you brought me into the case, I asked you to put everything on the table. I need you to do that. I'm walking a fine line here, involving a civilian in the case as it is. Our history can only go so far." Jake apologized and agreed to Rick's conditions.

"Do you have the contact information of the R.C.M.P. member you spoke to in New Denver?" Rick asked. Jake found his wallet, pulled out a business card and handed it to Rick. Rick picked up the phone and dialed the number. When he got hold of the member, he told him that Leonard was a person of interest in a kidnapping case, and if he saw him in the area, to contact him. The member replied that, as a matter of fact, he saw the man just last night. He was gassing up at around midnight. "Did he have anyone with him?" Rick asked. "There was an older guy in the passenger seat, didn't recognized him." "We'll get up there as soon as we can." Rick said, and then hung up the phone. Jake asked, "Can I borrow your computer for a minute?" "Go ahead." While Jake was on the computer, Rick called the Mounties back, "Can you arrange for a warrant for the Kohler property? We'll need the entire property, residence and any out buildings." "What specifically are we looking for?" the Mountie asked. "Kidnap victim Frank Compton." "Will try and have it here by the time you arrive." By the time Rick hung up, Jake had looked at the aviation weather. "Looks like good VFR weather for the next couple of days. The only airport in New Denver is a heliport, but there is one in Kaslo that's suitable. If you like, we can fly up in my plane and save a few hours each way." "I can get the Mounties to pick us up." Rick offered. He grabbed his Kevlar vest and police windbreaker and they headed for the parking lot.

As the two reached the car, Rick's cell phone rang, it was Steven. "It's almost noon, what are we supposed to do about the wire transfer?" "Just hold off for now. When they call back, if it's not Frank on the line, tell them you want proof of life. We're on our way to New Denver now so we just need to buy some time."

The two drove directly to Boundary Bay, where Jake prepped the plane for the flight, and filed his flight plan. "The flight should take us about two hours. We'll be at ninety-five hundred feet so we won't need oxygen." He plugged the coordinates into the GPS and took off.

After about an hour and fifteen minutes they were over Kelowna. The mountains were green and lush after the spring melt, but Jake knew in another month or so, green would turn to brown, as the temperatures rose, and sucked the moisture from the ground.

Rick never was comfortable in small planes. His idea of a small plane was a Dash Eight, anything smaller was just a toy. Forty-five minutes later, Kaslo appeared ahead of them. The airport was about a nautical mile west of the town. Rick spotted it first and Jake set up for the approach. They backtracked on the runway, and then onto the main apron. There wasn't much there, except for three small, private hangars, and a payphone. By the time Jake shut down, a police car was pulling into the small gravel parking lot beside the apron. "I'm constable Mike O'Brian, I've been asked to help you gents any way I can. Where would you like to go?" "How about the detachment for starters." Rick said.

When they got to the detachment, Mike introduced them to his staff sergeant, Ron Tkatchuk, and offered them coffee. "The search warrant came in about a half hour ago. Someone from New Denver will meet us at the farm with it." The sergeant told them. "Also, we requested a K-9 unit from Nelson as soon as we spoke to you, so they should be here any minute. Can we get you anything to eat while we're waiting?" Jake said, "I don't know about you Rick, but I could use a sandwich. I don't know when we might get another chance." Rick added, "Make it two."

While they waited, Rick briefed the Mounties on the case so far. The Kohler brothers and their friends, were well known to local police, and they were more than happy to cooperate in any way that would get them out of the community.

The K-9 team from Nelson arrived just as the pair was finishing their sandwiches. The team studied the satellite images of the property, and assigned areas to be searched. Constable O'Brian then handed Jake a Kevlar vest, and a blue windbreaker. The sergeant spoke up, "We'll take the lead on executing the search warrant. Rick you'll partner up with me, and Jake, you'll stay with Mike. Jake, because you're a civilian, I'm afraid you and Mike will bring up the rear. Are you clear on that?" Remembering his last encounter with Leonard, Jake replied, "No argument from me."   They loaded into three cars, and headed for the farm.

The ride there was pretty quiet. The team members were busy getting their heads into the game. When they pulled onto the property, the three cars fanned out as they had planned in the briefing. Two members approached the main house and announced themselves. Two more went to the barn, while the dog team moved around back of the main house and waited.

When nobody answered, they breached the door with a ram, and went inside. Within five minutes, the house had been cleared. The barn team did the same. This time, no trace of the guard dog. After both buildings were given the all clear, the sergeant motioned for Jake to join them. "Ok, we're going to spread out and cover the entire property. We're looking for any signs of a place, where a person, or persons could conceal themselves. Jake, you can shadow Mike." As they searched, the sun had started to drop in the west, and it began to cast late afternoon shadows. Jake was starting to get that uneasy feeling again. He shook it off as paranoia, after all he was in good company.

As they moved slowly up the path Jake and Carla had walked only days before, they came across the weapons range. Other than fresh four by four tracks, not much looked as if it had changed. The team continued into the woods, without seeing much of interest, and was finally stopped, when they hit a barbed wire fence at the property line. They retraced their steps back to the main trail leading away from the yard. Following it another hundred yards, there was another, smaller one, branching off to the left. It was apparent that there had been some recent traffic and activity in the area, but it didn't seem to go anywhere. Before they proceeded any further, and contaminated the area, the sergeant radioed for the dog handler to meet them. When he got there put the dog on a long leash, and started working him. It didn't take long before the dog picked up a fresh scent. The handler followed close behind until the dog stopped and yelped. He was sneezing continuously. "Assholes," the handler swore, "they've peppered the trail with cayenne. The dog is going to be useless for the rest of the day now." He took him back to the car, and returned to rejoined the team. "Why would they want their trail to stop here?" Mike asked, "It doesn't seem to go anywhere." "Good question." His sergeant replied. "Let's keep moving."

After about ten minutes, something out of the corner of Jake's eye caught his attention. The sun was reflecting off of the lens, of what looked like a surveillance camera, about ten feet up a tree. He was about to call out to the others, but thought better of it. Instead he quietly scanned the trees for signs of other cameras. Jake drew a mental map of its location. They continued for another fifteen minutes with no luck, as the path looped around to where it met up with the highway, about a quarter mile from the yard entrance. As they walked along the shoulder of the highway, Jake told the rest of the team about the camera. "It's quite possible we were being watched the whole time, and I didn't want them to know we were onto them." "Good thinking." They all agreed. Jake continued, "I'm assuming you guys have access to night vision, or infrared goggles. Maybe we could come back after dark, and take another look." The sergeant answered first. "Good plan. Let's head back to town, have some dinner, and regroup. We'll plan to be back, around twenty-one hundred. It should be getting dark by then."

As they drove back to Kaslo, a light drizzle started to fall. The thought of trudging around the forest in the rain, at night, was appealing to no one. Rick's cell phone broke the silence. It was Steven. "Dad just called and asked what was happening. He said if the money wasn't wired within the hour,   they   would   start sending body parts back to the family. They were able isolate the call from a cell tower east of New Denver." "We can't call their bluff, so you'll have to send it. Our priority is the victim, we can worry about trying to recover the money later." Rick told him. The team knew they were getting close. They just had to somehow get to Frank, before he lost his leverage, and outgrew his usefulness to the kidnappers.

Back in town, the entire team, with the exception of the dog team, who had departed back to Nelson, headed to a local café. Ron ordered his meal, and then walked over to the detachment, to check on things and make some calls. While the team was eating, Jake filled them in on events from the beginning. "The poor Compton's just can't catch a break. I feel bad if we, even inadvertently, had anything to do with it." Mike said. Just as they were finishing up, Ron walked back in the door. As he took his seat he said, "Great news, New Denver is sending a couple of their members, to assist us tonight. They'll meet us at the gate to the farm." When his meal came, Ron asked the waitress to box it to go, and they all headed back to the detachment.

The light drizzle had turned to a steady light rain, and the temperature had dropped noticeably. When they arrived back in the squad room, Mike rounded up the gear they would need for tonight's mission, two sets of night vision goggles and an infrared camera. He also equipped two rifles with night vision scopes. As the team refreshed themselves with the satellite photo, Jake pointed to where he saw the camera. Ron cautioned, "If there's one camera, there's a good chance there are others we missed, and they're probably night vision equipped. They didn't go through all this effort, and use cheap equipment, so keep that in mind when we're on site. Jake, did you notice if the camera had a red, active light on it?" "I didn't see one, but I only got a glance." "Ok," Ron continued, "We'll leave the New Denver car and one of their members on point, along the highway at the main gate. Mike, you and Jake will take point where the path comes out at the highway. You keep one set of night vision goggles. The rest of us will work our way along the path, where the camera was spotted, which seems to be an area they've deemed important enough to monitor. Hell, they certainly neutralized the dog team there. Mike, grab a portable spotlight. We can use it to neutralize the cameral if need be. Sunset tonight is twenty-one o three. We depart here at twenty-one hundred, which should put us at the Kohler's, by dark. Any questions?" None were put forward. "Ok, we have about thirty minutes before we head out, so take care of any business you need to tend to now."

Rick called back to Steven. "Did the transfer take place ok?" "As far as we know." Steven replied. "Good," Rick said, "don't get too eager, but we may have a lead on your dad's location. We're on our way shortly to check it out." "That's great news, I'll let mom know, she needs something to boost her spirits." "I'll call you when I have something to tell you." Rick told him, and hung up.

While Rick was on the phone to Steven, Jake called Carla. He updated their progress so far, and let her know that they were going back again tonight. She told him, "I kind of like what we have going here, so don't get yourself shot, or anything stupid like that." "Not to worry, constable Mike, my babysitter, and I are relegated to the perimeter, so not much chance of that. Mike's a nice enough guy, but if I have to sit in a car, at night, in the rain, in the middle of nowhere, I'd sooner it was with you."

"You just know how to win over a girl, don't you?" They both had a good chuckle and he hung up.

At twenty-one hundred, Ron stepped out of his office and told the team to load up and get ready to roll. "One last word, do I need to say it?" Jake chuckled to himself as, in unison, all the Mounties, and Rick, responded with, "be careful out there." He thought they only said that on cop shows.

Ron, Rick, and another constable rode in the lead car. Jake and Mike followed in the second. The steady light rain continued, and when the sun went down, the temperature dipped into the mid teens. The team in the lead car went over the plan one more time to make sure everyone was on the same page. The men in the second car, were expecting the night to be pretty quiet on their end.

As the cars approached the property, they could see in the distance another police car, this one, with its rooftop lights lit up. While Mike pulled his car up to their assigned point and stopped, Ron pulled up behind the flashing lights, and got out to approach the car. It was the two members, Jim and Pete, from New Denver. He jumped in the back of their patrol, car and they relayed what was happening. They had arrived at the property to meet up with the Kaslo team, and observed a truck pulling out from the main gate, so they decided to do a traffic stop, to get an identification. As they approached the vehicle, they noticed that it was the same man they saw earlier in the day, with Leonard. When they asked him for his driver's licence, he told them he didn't have it with him. He identified himself as Frank Compton. Ron asked the member, "Did he say anything about being kidnapped?" "No," he responded, "but that's when you guys came on scene, so maybe he didn't have a chance yet." Ron grabbed his portable, and called for Mike and Jake to join them. When they pulled alongside, Ron motioned for Jake to step out of the car and join him. As Jake walked up, he immediately recognized Frank, and Frank recognized Jake. Jake asked Frank, "What's going on?" Frank seemed a little shaken and confused. He took a minute to compose himself, and then uttered, "Thank God you found me." "Are you alright?" Jake asked him. "I think so." He answered.

The men moved Frank over to the police cruiser, and Ron told the team to stand by, while they sorted this all out. "How did you escape?" Rick asked him. "I didn't" he responded, "The guy holding me sent me to town for beer and cigarettes. He said if I wasn't back within an hour, he would hurt my family. That's where I was going when they pulled me over." "Where's the guy now?" Ron asked him. "He has an underground survival bunker, behind the house, off to the left of the main path." "That's were I saw the camera, and where the dog was disabled." Jake said. "Can you describe the bunker?" Ron jumped in. "It was about ten feet by ten feet, with cinder block walls and concrete floor and roof." "Where's the entrance?" "Under some spruce bows, a few yards off the path." Frank pointed to its position on the map. "It has a hinged steel plate door you lift up, and then climb down a ladder. The door can be barred from the inside so you won't get in, unless he unlocks it." "Did you see any weapons?" Ron continued. "He has a handgun and some high powered rifles. He also has a monitor in there, so he can see anyone approaching. We saw you this afternoon. He's a scary guy. He kept muttering he would die before he ends up like his brother. I don't know what he meant by that." "His brother's in jail."

Jake replied. "Another thing," Frank added, "He has enough food and water to last him a couple of weeks." "Did you see a dog?" Rick asked him. "Yes, he has one, but some greasy looking, biker type, came over this morning and took him." "One less thing to worry about." Ron piped in.

Frank asked if it was ok to call his family. Ron agreed but told him to keep it short for now.

Rick and Ron came up with a new plan of attack. "We're going to need your jacket and cap." Ron told Frank. "We'll give it another thirty minutes, so the timing to New Denver and back is right. I'll go in from the main path wearing Frank's coat and cap. It's dark, so hopefully, he won't recognize that it's not actually Frank. Rick, you and Jim will come around the back way, from where the path comes out to the highway. That's where Mike and Jake will be on point. Pete, you stay on point, at the main gate with Frank. We'll maintain radio silence once I head in. We're going for a simple bust here. If he barricades, or the shit hits the fan, we back off, and bring the Emergency Response Team. Questions?" Everyone was good.

When it was nearing thirty minutes, Ron jumped into the truck Frank had been driving, and pulled into the yard, while the other two cars, took up their point positions. It was raining harder now, and the wind had come up, to the point, where the rustling trees made it almost deafening. Ron walked toward the bunker at a deliberate pace, while Rick and Jim cautiously worked their way from the other direction. When they were about a hundred feet from the bunker, they held their position. Scanning the area with their night vision goggles they waited for Ron. As he appeared on the path, the men kept their goggles trained on him, waiting on his signal. If the mood wasn't tense enough, the sound of the wind and rain, masked any chance of hearing any potential danger approaching . With rain running down their faces and into their eyes, it was hard maintaining any kind of clear vision. By the time Ron reached the entrance to the bunker, Rick and Jim had their rifles off safety, and trained on the bushes guarding it. Jim pulled his jacket over his head, trying to protect the scope, from rain getting on the lenses, and his eyes. It helped. As Ron readied to swing the metal plate that covered the entrance, he pulled out his side arm. Jim could see clearly through the scope, as Ron raised his left hand, with three fingers showing, to count down with. As he lowered each finger one at a time, to a fist, he tugged at the plate, gently at first, to test it. When he determined that it wasn't locked, he threw it open completely. A voice from inside yelled out, "Frank, is that you?" Ron replied back, "Police, come out with your hands on top of your head, fingers clasped." He barely got his last words out when a shot rang out, and echoed through the night air. Rick and Jim were already rushing toward Ron, and the bunker. They took up positions flanking Ron, so no one was in the crossfire. All weapons were trained on the entrance. He repeated, "Leonard, there's no where to go, put down your gun, and come up the ladder, now." His demand was answered by another round. Jim passed Ron a loaded tear gas gun. He crawled up as close to the entrance hole as he safely could, raised himself to his knees and fired one round into the bunker. The canister exploded, and a gray smoke started to billow from the opening. Leonard climbed the ladder and Rick saw it first. "Gun, gun, gun." He yelled. Leonard had donned a gas mask, and had an automatic handgun in his right hand. As his head and shoulders cleared the entrance, he let go two rounds, at no particular target. The three cops responded, with a dozen of their own. Leonard   disappeared   again below the entrance, and there was silence. Jim tossed Ron the only gas mask they had with them, then he and Rick held their positions, while Ron pulled it on, and inched his way to the edge of the hole. He slowly raised up, arms extended in the ready position. The smoke was starting to clear now. The wind didn't take long to carry the effects of the gas, to the other two, who weren't protected. The acrid taste came first, and then the burning eyes. They quickly moved up wind of the bunker, to be out of it. Ron's eyes never left the bunker, as he became more and more exposed. Except for the wind and the rain, it was silent. Her could feel his heart, pounding in his chest. Finally, he could see a limp shape, at the bottom of the ladder. It was Leonard, and he wasn't moving. He waived the other two men over to a position on the upwind side of the entrance, so they could cover him. Ron holstered his weapon, and carefully climbed down the ladder, keeping his eyes trained on his suspect. When he reached the bottom, he could see that several of the shots, had found their target. The gun lay beside Leonard, and Ron quickly kicked it away. He bent over him and checked him for a pulse. He felt nothing. Ron climbed back up the ladder, joined the other two men, and took off his mask. "Go ahead and radio the point units, and let them know we're all clear, subject down. Have them hold their positions, we need to secure the scene, until the shooting team arrives." He pulled his cell phone out of his pocket, and called E Division headquarters in Surrey. "They'll have a team up hear by sunup." He told the others. Ron dialed the Kaslo detachment and told them to send a couple members to help with the scene. "Pick up sandwiches and hot coffee, it's going to be a long, cold, night." When the relief members arrived, Ron sent Mike back to Kaslo with Jake, Rick and Frank.

It was close to midnight when they arrived back at the detachment. Mike arranged for motel rooms for the three men. He told them, "Look, it's late, get some rest, and be back at eight o'clock, so we can get your statements." When they got to their respective rooms, Frank called his family, while Jake called Carla.

He had obviously woken her up. He could hear the grogginess, mixed with panic, in her voice. "How are you?" Jake asked. "More importantly, how are you?" Carla threw it back at him. "I'm fine. Look I can't go into details right at this moment, but I wanted to let you know, everything is ok on this end. You'll probably hear it on the news by morning, Leonard was fatally shot tonight." "Oh my God, were you involved?" "Fortunately no, I was back at a point position on the highway, with one of the local members. I heard the shots, but that's as close to the action as I got." "How are you taking it?" She asked him. "A bit shaken up, but I'll be ok. It's not something you come across much in the corporate world." "Stay safe, and I'll see you when you get back." Carla closed with. From Frank's room, the conversation went much the same.

CHAPTER ELEVEN

None of the trio slept much through the night. By seven o'clock, they were at Café Lago, ordering breakfast. Jake and Frank were numb from the whole experience, but Rick had been there many times. He assured them, that what they felt now, was normal, and that they would start feeling more like themselves, quite quickly. They seemed to take comfort in that. The men finished up, and walked over to the detachment, at about ten to eight. At least the rain had stopped sometime during the night, and it looked as though the clouds were starting to break up. Jake thought this was good news, they would be able to fly out today.

When they got to the detachment, Mike was already at a computer, updating the file.

"Gentlemen," he said to them, "how was the motel, comfortable I trust?" They all nodded as Jake spoke. "No complaints." "Grab any desk that's free, and I'll come over and bring up a statement form, on the computer." Jake's statement was quite short. Not much to report on, when you're just sitting at a point position. Rick's report took much longer, because of his involvement in the events. Frank's was the lengthiest as he had to account for the entire time, he was a kidnap victim. When he was finished, Mike printed it, and reviewed it.

In essence, he told of the morning he was kidnapped, seven days ago. The only person he saw during the whole time, was his captor. Leonard kept them moving around for a couple of days, and they made the calls to the family, from different points around Vancouver. They spent two nights at the Holiday Inn downtown. They would have stayed longer, but Jake spotted Leonard in the lobby. After that they left town immediately and came to the farm. He went on to say, that Leonard made other calls from his cell phone, but he didn't know whom they were to. When the police came to the property the first time, they were already in the bunker. After police left, Leonard wasn't expecting them back, but they stayed put just to be certain. Leonard wanted beer and cigarettes, but was worried the police were looking for him. That's when he sent Frank into town, and when he was pulled over on the highway. Mike handed it back to him and asked him to date, and sign it. "Mike," Rick asked, "could you make a copy of Frank's statement for our file?" "No problem." As he copied all the statements, and gave them to Rick.

As he was signing the statement, Ron walked through the door. He had stayed at the scene, and waited for the shooting team, who arrived just before sun up. They took over the scene, and after they had a look around, let Ron back into the bunker. When he was in there the first time, he couldn't see much except for smoke. By morning, the smoke was gone, and only a hint of gas remained. Not enough to incapacitate, but certainly enough make a person uncomfortable after a few minutes. What he saw was alarming. The bunker was well stocked with water, mainly dehydrated food, and other supplies. Leonard could have held up for weeks. The frightening part, was he had a small, but effective armory down there. If not for Frank, it would have been almost impossible, to have found the entrance. Ron read over the men's statements, and told them, "Good job everyone involved. The detectives will probably have more questions for you, but they will get in touch directly. Thanks for your help, you can head home whenever you're ready."

Mike drove Jake, Rick, and Frank to the airport. The clouds had scattered out nicely. Jake called Flight Services for a weather briefing, and the entire route home looked good, so he filed his flight plan, did his pre-flight checks, and they were airborne fifteen minutes later.

Carla was keeping busy on her end. After she got the news from Jake she started preparing her motion to dismiss the case against the Compton's. She got hold of the federal prosecutor, and gave him a heads up. Steven had left first thing, to pick up his family in Whistler. It was all over.

After a couple of hours airborne, they were on final approach to Boundary Bay. For Jake, returning home always felt good, but this time it felt particularly special, and it didn't have anything to do with their ordeal.

CHAPTER TWELVE

When Jake taxied up to his tie down area, and shut down, Rick told Frank, to come with him to headquarters, so he could make a statement for the Vancouver Police Department, as they were the agency that opened the original file. In another fifteen minutes, Jake had the plane secured, and was on his way to Carla's office. The drive, this time of day, took him about forty-five minutes. It seemed like a lifetime. He found a parking spot, a few doors down from her office. When Jake walked into the reception area, Carla's assistant announced him. She came out of her office and escorted him back in. After she closed the door, she wrapped her arms around him, and planted a long, lingering kiss, catching him totally off

101

guard. He was happy to reciprocate. "Are you hungry?" Carla asked him. "Now that you mentioned it, yes." "The best sandwiches in town, are only a block from here, lets go." Hubbub Sandwiches and Salads, was one of the best-rated delis in Vancouver. Carla and her assistant, ordered from there, at least twice a week. When they arrived, it wasn't very busy. Most of the lunch crowd had already come and gone. They both ordered the pulled pork sandwiches, and Jake wasn't disappointed. "I know you were only gone overnight, but I missed you." Carla told him. "God, now I'm sounding like a clingy school girl." She added. "Well, believe it or not, I had way too much time to think, just sitting in a police car waiting, for something to happen. And what I thought most about, was you." "Right answer." Carla replied, laughing. When they had finished lunch, Jake walked Carla back to her office, gave her a quick kiss on the sidewalk, got into his car and headed for his own office.

He stood in his doorway and looked around the room. It was only a couple of days, but it felt like eons since he was here last. So much had happened, in such a short time. He sat down behind his desk, reached into the bottom right hand drawer, and pulled out the bottle of Louis XIII, he kept there, to celebrate his first big case. There was no question, this one qualified. He found a relatively clean coffee cup, blew the dust out, broke the seal on the bottle, and poured himself a double. As he sat there, by himself, with the only light, entering from the window, he realized, he hadn't felt this alive in a long time. When the cup was empty he picked up his phone. "Carla, it's just me again, unless you have a better offer, can I cook dinner for you tonight?" "That's a great offer, shall I bring red or white?" "Let's go with red." He replied. "Oh, one other thing," she asked, "could you contact Rick and your R.C.M.P buddy, and get me whatever reports you can from them? I'll need them for my motion to dismiss." "Sure, I'll call him right away, and I'll see you around seven, if that works." "It works, see you then."

Jake picked up the phone again and dialed Rick. "Hello Rick, it's Jake." "Glad you called," Rick answered, "I just got back from dropping Frank at home. I got his statement, but I'm going to need one from you as well." "I thought you might." Jake said. "If you're going to be around for bit, I can be there in twenty minutes." "That would be great." "Also, Carla's filing a motion to dismiss the U.S. court case, and asked if you could provide as much of the case file, as possible." "Sure, I can put that together while you're writing your statement. See you in twenty." Jake's next call was to Peter McDaniel at the Burnaby detachment. Peter was pretty much up to speed on the incident. News of any officer involved shooting, travels fast. He agreed to send Jake at least a summary of the file, in the next day or two. Jake thanked him, locked up and drove to police headquarters. Rick set him up at a computer and he wrote up his statement, pretty much identical, as the one he gave in Kaslo. When he was done, Rick handed him a brown envelope, with the files he needed for Carla. "Look Rick, I really appreciate all you've helped me with on this one. As soon as we dispose of the court case, Carla and I will take you and your wife out for dinner. We haven't had much time to really catch up, have we?" "Looking forward to it, just give us a call when you're ready." Rick replied.

Jake drove directly to the market, where he picked up fresh penne, garlic, and basil. He found a couple of cans of whole tomatoes, a head of Romaine lettuce, and a loaf of fresh Italian bread. Dinner would be simple and fresh. Home cooked meals were few and far between, these days it seemed. He beat Carla to the condo by minutes. When she arrived she had two bottles of Merlot, and an overnight bag. Jake smiled, "Moving in?" "No, just don't want to have to drive, after a few glasses of wine." "There are taxis you know." He said laughing. "That can easily be arranged." She said, laughing with him.

Jake threw all the ingredients into a pot, and added some seasoning. "This will take about forty-five minutes, I'm running a little late, so if you don't mind keeping an eye on it, I'll grab a shower." "Ok, I'll open the wine and let it breath." She offered. While Jake was in the shower, Carla found an FM station, playing light jazz. She turned the volume down low, and set the table. Jake walked into the kitchen, looking much fresher, than he did twenty minutes before. Carla poured him a glass of wine, and offered him a toast, with the one she had already poured for herself. Jake got busy putting together a Caesar salad, while Carla, sliced the bread. He tested the sauce, that was simmering slowly. "Almost ready." He declared. He filled a large pasta pot, with water, and lit another burner. When the water boiled, he dropped the pasta in. "Dinner in four minutes." He announced.

After dinner, Jake made espressos, and the couple retired to the living room. The combination of wine, along with the soft music, couldn't help but set romantic mood. "Do I really need to call a taxi?" Carla asked, like a good lawyer, already knowing the answer. He took her by the hand and led her toward the bedroom. On the way, she grabbed her bag, and told him, "Let me change into something more appropriate." "By all means, don't take too long." He said. As she went into the bathroom, Jake got undressed and slipped under the covers. Ten minutes later Carla stood in the bathroom doorway, the light from behind her, shone through her sheer nightie, and highlighted a body, that could have easily belonged to a twenty year old. Jake was fast asleep. She let out a sigh, and quietly crawled in beside him. Disappointed yes, but there was no way she could be angry.

CHAPTER THIRTEEN

It had been a full week since they returned from Kaslo. Within forty-eight hours, news of it all, had hit the both local, and national media. The headlines read: ***Retired accountant arrested in Washington state, for smuggling drugs in a boat bought from police.*** The story went on to read: *"A local Vancouver couple got more than they bargained for..."* It was slanted more like a human-interest story, than actual news. The kidnapping and shooting, were almost a footnote. It just reinforced his distain for the press. Jakes name was mentioned in the article, and his phone didn't stop ringing for two days. At least the publicity, would probably help advance his private practice.

The Compton's had settled their bill with Jake, and he was officially off the clock. Frank and Margaret's preliminary hearing, was set for that afternoon. Carla was satisfied with the files she had received, and was confident they would support her motion. Steven had offered his wife's seven-passenger van, for the drive down to Seattle. That way all five of them could go in one vehicle. They met at Jakes office at eight in the morning. That would give them plenty of time, for the three-hour drive, even if the Douglas border crossing was backed up.

While they drove, the group talked about everything, but the ordeal they had just been through. Carla had settled back into her normal day-to-day routine. Jake had a couple of quiet days after the media storm, before he got some surveillance work from one of his corporate contacts. Frank and Margaret decided to take a few weeks, and continue down the coast, with the boat. The marina manager had found a used Catalina keel, and was ready to install it, as soon as the boat was released back to the Compton's. They had already shut down the house, and Steven would keep an eye on it, in their absence. The border crossing went uneventful, which gave them plenty of time for a short rest stop. They found a coffee shop just off the I-5 in Bellingham, and pulled in, used the facilities, grabbed coffees to go, and were back on the interstate in fifteen minutes.

The group arrived at the Federal Court building on Stewart Street, by eleven thirty. That gave them two hours before they were due in court.

Steven punched "restaurants" into the GPS. They had lots of time, so he skipped over fast food places, and found Barolo's, a block away. He found a parking spot across the street from the courthouse, and they walked to the restaurant from there.

They were able to have a leisurely lunch. Everyone was in relaxed mood. Even, surprisingly, Frank and Margaret. Carla had couriered copies of her documents, to the prosecutor, so he should have reviewed them prior to the hearing. She was expecting a fairly short appearance. Jake looked at the time, it was one-ten. "Time to go." He announced. Steven looked after the bill, and they headed toward the courthouse.

Once inside, Carla checked the docket, to see which courtroom they were booked in. Once they found it, they found seats, and waited for the judge to enter. At precisely one thirty, the clerk called "All rise," and the judge entered, and took his seat at the bench. They waited, as the court heard two cases before theirs. When the clerk called their case, Carla, Frank, and Margaret, walked through the swinging gate, at the front of the pews, and took their seats at the defense table. The judge addressed them, "I've read the defenses motion to dismiss, do you have anything additional to add at this time?" "No your honor." Carla responded. "Prosecution?" "No your honor. In light of the evidence the defense has put forth, the prosecution is withdrawing the charges." The judge declared, "The charges are withdrawn without prejudice. I'm sorry you had to endure these unfortunate circumstances. You are free to go." He turned his attention to the court clerk, "Would you see to it that their property is released, forthwith." "I'll make those arrangements immediately your honor." She replied.

They left the courtroom, escorted by the prosecutor, who led them downstairs to the clerk's office. He had already arranged for the paperwork, so in another ten minutes, the five of them were walking out of the building. "I know it was just a formality, but hearing the judge make it official, lifted a huge weight off our shoulders." He added, "I really want to thank both you Jake, and you Carla, for all your help in this. It could have gone south very easily." "Glad we were able to arrive at the outcome that we did." Carla replied. "Frank asked, "Do you mind if Steven drops us off at the downtown ferry terminal before you head back? We'll catch the Victoria Clipper to Friday Harbor." He looked at Jake, "Do you know of a good place on the island to spend a night?" Jake looked over at Carla, and grinned. "As a matter of fact I do." When they were dropped off at the ferry terminal on Alaskan Way, they said their goodbyes, Steven told them to stay in touch, and the three of them headed back for Vancouver. The ride home was quiet.

CHAPTER FOURTEEN

A week had passed since the court appearance. Jake and Carla were busy on separate cases, so they hadn't had the opportunity to spend much time together. Carla dialed his number. "Do you have any plans this weekend?" she asked him. "Not at all, what did you have in mind?" "Why don't we get out of the city? We could go up to the condo in Whistler." "Best offer I've had all week." Jake replied. "Great, how about I pick you up Friday around four, and we can be up there in time for dinner." "I can't wait." He told her. "Can I make a reservation somewhere?" "That would be nice, you choose." She told him. They hung up. Friday was only a day away, but Jake couldn't wait for it to get there. He went on-line and searched, fine dining in Whistler. Araxi looked like it would do quite well.

Friday arrived with a clear sky, and warm forecast all the way up the pacific coast. Jake was like a kid at Christmas, four o'clock couldn't get there quick enough. He got to the office by nine. He checked his messages and returned some calls. His surveillance case was coming to an end, and he was busy finishing his report, about an employee, claiming a work related injury. What ever the injury was, it didn't seem to interfere with his daily round of golf. When he had finished it, he picked up the phone and called Rick. When it was answered, Jake reminded him, "Hey, I still owe you a dinner, does next weekend work for you and your wife?" "Sure, I think Saturday's open." "Terrific, I'll confirm with Carla, and get back to you by Wednesday." He busied himself tidying up his office. That only killed a half hour, so he walked over to Starbuck's and ordered a cappuccino. When he had finished, he started for home.

Carla was running a few minutes late, but Jake was elated to see her. They embraced, and were tempted not to release, but they had all weekend to get lost in each other. "Why don't we take the Jag?" Jake offered. "It's such a beautiful day, I'll put the top down." "I'd like that." Carla replied, thinking the entire time, "there goes a two hundred dollar hairstyle. Oh well, it'll be worth it."

During the drive up, they kept the conversation light, mainly catching up on personal topics, general likes and dislikes. For as long as they had known each other, they realized there were a lot of things they had never spoken about. He knew she liked jazz, but what else did she like? What were their favorite colors, favorite foods? Not earth shattering topics, but all part of really getting to know someone. The conversation flowed easily, and before either of them realized, they were pulling into Whistler. Jake had made the reservation for eight, so it gave them time to get settled in to the condo, and have a glass of wine, before they left for dinner. Carla's condo, was just on the edge of the village. Everything was within walking distance. A little before eight they worked their way to the restaurant. The mountain air was cooling down as the sun was starting to set, but it was clean, and filled with the aroma of pine trees. It reminded Jake of the events, of only a couple of weeks ago. He shook off the thought, and kept walking.

It was Friday night, so the restaurant was full. He gave the hostess his name, and she took them straight to their table. He had never eaten there, but Carla was familiar with the place. "Good choice." She told him. They looked over the wine list, and decided to let the Sommelier surprise them. Both opted out of appetizers, and just ordered their meals. Jake was feeling good, and decided to go with the New York steak, while Carla ordered Roast Loin of Venison.

They ate their meals slowly, talking as they went. "I know the case is over and I'm off the clock, but there's still a couple things about it, that just keep coming back." Jake said. "Are you sure it's not just paranoia?" Carla replied. "Probably." Jake answered. "Why don't you use me as a sounding board, maybe the lawyer in me can make some sense of it." "First off," he said, "I understand using Frank's cell phone to contact his family, but why use it to contact other people. I'm certain Leonard would have at least a burner phone. Also, Leonard said they spent a couple of nights at the Holiday Inn.

When Rick and I checked with the manager, he told us there was no Kohler registered. They couldn't have used a fake name because they would have had to show picture ID. And what's with the all moving around anyhow? Wouldn't staying put, reduce the risk of the victim escaping, or being seen? Another thing, I would think kidnappers would be anxious, and try to get the ransom, as quick as possible. Leonard didn't appear to be in much of a hurry, as he dragged it out for almost a week. The big one is, you met Crusher, the guy at the farm, with the shotgun. When I met Leonard in the parking garage, I could tell he and Crusher were cut from the same cloth. Do they look like the type, sophisticated enough to set up, and orchestrate money transfers to an offshore account? I doubt if they even have accounts at their local Credit Union." Carla thought about his points, then offered, "All good points. As individual points, I wouldn't put too much importance on any of them, and would chalk it up to over thinking. But, when you string them all together, I think a closer look may be warranted. You're right about these guys. I think most of the people around there, are intelligent, hard working folks, but I think the Kohler brothers and their pals, are swimming in the shallow end of the gene pool, so to speak."   Jake stopped her there. "Sorry I even brought up the subject tonight. Let's just focus on you and me for the rest of the weekend." "Agreed, that's what Monday to Friday is for." She responded, and they focused on the rest of their dinner. When their server came by and asked them about desert or coffee, they just ordered coffees. Jake said, "Just decaf for me, I don't want to be up all night." As soon as the woman left, Carla whispered in his ear, "coffee keeping you up all night, will be the least of your worries." He thought to himself, "every time she speaks, he becomes more attracted to her."

They finished their coffees, and strolled back to the condo. Even though it was a ski resort, in the summer, the village was vibrant with activity, and you couldn't help but get drawn into its atmosphere. Carla lit the gas fireplace while Jake poured them each a glass of wine. They sat quietly, snuggled together, on the thick faux sheepskin carpet in front of the sofa, and were hypnotized by the flames. When their wine was gone, Jake stood up, and held his arms out to help Carla up. She went straight to the bedroom, while Jake stopped only long enough to refill their glasses.

The rest of the weekend was every bit as fulfilling as that night. When they left on Sunday evening, they were both more relaxed and content, than either had been in many years. They looked forward to many more just like it.

CHAPTER FIFTEEN

Jake's head was still in the clouds, when he drove to his office Monday morning. Time to focus on earning a paycheck. His mind kept drifting back to what they spoke about briefly, at dinner Friday night. There was nothing pressing on his calendar, so he got back into his car and drove to the Holiday Inn. He parked in the passenger drop off zone, and went into the lobby, and up to the front desk, where he asked for the manager. A couple of minutes passed, and manager emerged from his office. "I don't know if you remember me." Jake said, "I was in here a few weeks ago, with detective Boiko." "Sure, sure, I remember. You were looking to see if a particular guest was registered. Any luck locating him?" the man

119

asked. "We eventually did catch up with him." Jake said, not going into any further detail. "I wonder if you could help me one more time? "I'm chasing down a hunch. I wonder if you wouldn't mind checking the register again, on or about the same date we asked about last time, but this time look for a Frank Compton." "Give me a second. I'll see what I can find." He logged on to the computer at the front desk, and looked up the date. "There he is, single room, two queens, two nights." He wrote down the information, and handed it to Jake. "Again, I really appreciate your cooperation, thank you."

Jake returned to his car and just sat there thinking. His job with the Compton's was done. Was he obligated legally, or morally, to pursue this information. He needed his sounding board, so he called her. She said, "Come on over to the office, I'll put a fresh pot on." When he got there, he had to drive around the block a couple of times until a parking spot opened up. As he walked in the office door, Carla's assistant told him, "Go right in, she's expecting you. Oh, and what happened this weekend, she's been humming all morning?" "I have no idea what you're talking about." He answered, not being able to look her in the eye, and still keep a straight face. Carla stood up and came around to the front of her desk when he walked through the door. She gave him a hug and told him to have a seat. She took the other one, beside him. Her assistant brought in the coffee, and closed the door on her way out. "Is this about what we discussed at supper the other night?" "Yes," he replied. "I did a little digging this morning, and found out it was Frank who had registered them at the Holiday Inn, and I don't know what my obligations are now." "Well, first off, from a legal point of view, you're not an officer of the court, so I don't see any issues there. You did your job in good faith. If there was anything illegal going on, you weren't part of it. Morally, so what if he registered them. He may have been forced into it, with direct threats to him or his family. Isn't that what he's maintained all along?" "That's true, but I would think he would have had plenty of opportunities, to escape, or signal for help, if that was the case." Carla told him, "You could ignore it and go back to your business, and no one could fault your for it. Or, and this may sound odd, coming from a defense lawyer, you could pursue justice, and find out the truth. You have to follow you own moral compass." "I know what you're saying," he said, "but at the end of the day, I still have to live with myself. Believe it or not, you have been a big help. I just have some soul searching to do." He thanked her, gave her quick kiss and left her office. Carla knew what he would do, even before he did. It's one of the things that had attracted her to him.

By the time he had walked to his car, Jake had made his decision. "Rick, are you at headquarters?" he said into his phone. "Ya, just pushing paper, what's up?" "If you have a few minutes, I'd like to drop by, and run a couple of things by you." "You bet, I could use the break. Come on over."

Traffic was light, and it didn't take him long to get there. When he got there and found Rick, Jake asked if there was somewhere quiet they could talk. There was no privacy in the bullpen. Rick led him to a small conference room, and pointed to a chair. "Can I get you anything?" Rick offered. "No, I'm fine, but thanks for asking. Jake basically repeated the conversation he and Carla had at the restaurant. Rick nodded, and understood what he was saying. He agreed with the gist of what Carla had said. "One on one, the points you made, really didn't seem that significant, but chained together, they may paint a different picture." "There may be something to it, maybe not. We're a little stretched here right now, but if you want to pursue it from your end, I'll give you whatever support I can from here." Rick said. "I'll take whatever I can get." Jake replied. "Could you contact sergeant Tkatchuk in Kaslo? See if, now that Leonard's dead, his buddy Charles can add anything of interest." "I'll call him right away." Rick said.

By the time Jake left police headquarters he was comfortable with his decision. He was really hoping it was nothing but overthinking, but this way he would sleep knowing he had done everything in his power, to find the truth. On his way back to his office, Jake grabbed a sandwich and a can of Coke, and had lunch at his desk. He decided to give Steven a call. When he answered, Jake asked him, "How are you doing?" "Pretty good. Everything's back to normal." "Normal's good." Jake replied. "Have you heard from your folks?" "As a matter of fact, I spoke with them two days ago. They're in San Diego. They found some dock space on Shelter Island across from the San Diego Yacht Club, and are in no hurry to return." "That's great news," Jake replied, "they've earned it. Tell them hello from Carla and me, next time you speak to them." "I sure will." And they said they're goodbyes.

Jake decided to call Peter, in Burnaby. When Peter finally picked up, Jake asked him, "I assume Lyle Kohler has been notified about his brother. Who did the notification, was it your guys, or the Department of Corrections?" "It would have been D.O.C." he answered. "Why" Jake gave Pete, the Reader's Digest version of what he discussed, with Carla and Rick. "I just wanted to find out, what his reaction was, or if he said anything, that might support the idea of something else going on." "Couldn't tell you, but if you like, I could take a run up to Agassiz, and interview him. Would that be of any help?" "It sure would." Jake said. "Alright, I'll head up in the morning, and should be able to get back to you by late afternoon."

The rest of the afternoon was spent returning calls from people looking for an investigator. Three suspected cheating spouses, parents wanting a background check on their son's fiancé, and an adopted woman looking for her birth mother. At least his name was out there now. He looked forward to the day, when he could pick and choose his clients, but for now, he'd take what was offered. Jake was able to set up five appointments at his office for tomorrow. He would at least evaluate each case, before he accepted or turned them down.

It was only mid-afternoon, but he decided to knock off for the day. A perk of self-employment. A pizza, a six pack of beer, and his night was planned. When he got home, he set the pizza box down on the coffee table, cracked a beer, and scanned the television channels, for a ball game. At about eight he called Carla and updated her about his meeting with Rick, and his call to Pete. She was happy, that was the decision he went with. She could tell by his voice, that he was too. "I almost forgot," he said, "are you available Saturday night for dinner with friends?" "That would be nice, I'd love to." "Great, I'll confirm, and get back to you." "You know," She added, "we don't always have to wait for a weekend, to get together." "I agree, how about Wednesday night? I'll find a bar with live music, and we'll grab some pub food, and a couple of drinks." "It sounds fun, I'm up for that." "Let me work on it, and I'll call you tomorrow." They said goodnight, he cracked another beer, and picked up the game again, in the seventh inning.

Pete arrived at Kent Institution, a little before ten the next morning. He had called ahead, and spoke to the warden, arranging the interview. When he entered the receiving area, he cleared his weapon, and locked it in one of the gun lockers reserved for law enforcement visitors. He was directed through a metal detector and given a pat down. Once he was signed in and given a visitors pass, a corrections officer escorted him to an interview room. The room was about ten feet by ten feet, no windows. There was a small metal table, bolted to the concrete floor, in the centre of the room. Three folding chairs were placed around it. The only other object in the room, was a closed circuit security camera, near the top of one wall. Pete took a seat in one of the chairs, put his notebook on the table, and waited for them to bring in Lyle. About five minutes later, the same corrections officer, returned with his inmate. He sat Lyle down, and attached his handcuffs, to a steel ring, welded to one edge of the table. "Just knock when you're done." He told Pete, as he walked out, and closed the door.

"Lyle, I just want you to know, I'm real sorry about Leonard. It's not what we had hoped to go down." Pete started with. Lyle sat silently, looking at his hands. "If you don't mind, I'd like to ask you a few questions." He continued. "Why would I help you?" Lyle asked him, not adjusting his gaze. "Well, we'd like to get the truth on how and why, this all happened. Don't you think Leonard deserves that much?" "Leonard's dead, what difference does it make?" Lyle responded. "You're right," Pete said, "It won't bring him back, but we can make sure justice is served on his behalf." There was no further response from Lyle. Pete kept going. "Do you recognize the name Frank Compton?" Lyle's eyes jumped from his hands, to peering directly into Pete's eyes. He held them there for one or two seconds, before they went back to his hands. "Never heard of the guy." He replied unconvincingly. "If you know this guy, or anything about what Leonard was involved in, give his memory enough respect, to help us find out the straight goods." "I can't help you, I want to go back to my cell now." Pete got up and knocked a couple of times on the door. The C.O. came in, and unshackled Lyle, from the table. As he was being led away, Pete handed Lyle a business card and said, "If you ever want to talk, please call me." Pete knew the man would ever call, but he always liked to leave the door open.

When he got back to the reception area, he claimed his gear, turned in his visitor's pass and left. It was about three o'clock by the time he got back to Burnaby. His first call was to Jake.

"Well, did you find anything out?" Jake asked anxiously. "Yes and no." Pete replied. "Lyle wasn't in much of a talking mood. When I mentioned Frank Compton's name, he denied knowing the guy. But, his involuntary reaction, told me a whole different story. There's some kind of connection there, I certain of it." Jake thanked him, and promised to keep him in the loop, then hung up the phone.

<h1 style="text-align:center">CHAPTER SIXTEEN</h1>

Two full weeks had passed, before Rick got back to Jake, about Charlie Hackford. Apparently he had been on vacation in Mexico. "Sorry it took so long," Rick told him, "but he just returned a couple of days ago" The Kaslo boys spoke to him, and are satisfied he had nothing to do with the kidnapping. He kept an eye on the farm while Leonard was in Vancouver, but that's about it. Charlie did say something that may be of interest to you. He said the Kohler brothers talked about a retired accountant in Vancouver, that helped them manage their money, though he had never met him." "Is this guy reliable, he didn't look like the type that would volunteer any information to police, when I had the pleasure of meeting him?" Jake asked him. "They seem to believe he's being straight with them. "Leonard's dead, he's got no reason to lie." "Do you see where I'm going with this?" Jake asked Rick. "I think it's enough of a coincidence to follow up on." Rick told him. "I'll keep you informed if I find anything else." They hung up and Jake dialed Steven's number.

"Good morning." He said to Steven, when he answered. They chatted the usual small talk for a minute, and then Jake asked him, "Have you heard from Frank and Margaret lately?" "Not since I last spoke with you. That's not like them, I'm starting to get concerned." Steven said. "Look, I'm just tying up loose ends," Jake added, "Do you know anything about his current clients?" "Not at all. That's a strange question, why do you ask?" " I'm just trying to be thorough." "I do know, that since he retired, he did keep a handful of clients, just to keep his hand in." "Ok, thanks. If you don't hear from him soon, don't hesitate to call me." Jake offered. "I won't." Steven said, and they hung up. Jake wasn't sure where to go from here. What he really wanted, was to get a look at Frank's client files, but he doubted that Frank would give him permission to look at confidential files, even if there was nothing to hide. He couldn't even think of asking Steven, until if, and when, he came to him for help. All he could do for now, was wait.

The wait was a short one. Next morning Steven called him back. "Jake," he said, "I may need your help again. Mom and Dad's cell phone just goes strait to voice mail when I call. The last time I spoke with them, they were in San Diego, somewhere near the San Diego Yacht Club. I'm not even sure where to start." "I think I still have the boat's registration number, but do you know what they named it?" Jake asked. "They named the boat, "Bean Counter." Steven told him. "Not original, but appropriate, I guess." Was all Jake could say. Leave it with me, and I'll see what I can find out. I'll call as soon as I have anything." "Thanks." Steven replied.

As soon as they hung up, Jake searched on-line, for marinas in San Diego. He found out that there was only about a half dozen or so marinas in the San Diego area, and only two of them were adjacent the Yacht Club, Kona Kai, and Shelter Cove, both situated on Shelter Island. He called Shelter Cove first, no luck.

When he called Kona Kai, they knew the boat right away. "Have you seen the owners around, in the last few days?" Jake asked the woman. "No, they paid a year up front for their slip, and said they were going travelling for a while." "I don't suppose they mentioned where?" he asked. "Afraid not." She replied. Jake thanked the woman for her help, gave her his number, and asked if she would call him, if they returned.

He was about to call Steven back, but thought the better of it. It was a dirty trick, but he wanted Steven to get a bit more stressed, so he could use his emotions, to get access to his father's files. He would call in the morning.

Jake and Carla had been seeing quite a lot of each other over the last two weeks, and they had both known for a while now, that things were getting serious. They just hadn't admitted it to each other. He felt that time was coming soon though . He called her, and they set dinner plans. Nowhere fancy, this would be part work, and part play. Pizza sounded good.

Pizza Guys was not far from Carla's office, so Jake parked out front, and they walked the few blocks to the restaurant. After they sat down, and ordered, Jake asked if he could run a couple things by her. "Of course." She answered. "I've worked cheap before, but I don't think I've ever been paid in pizza." "I'll sweeten the deal with wine." Jake said. He went on to tell her about the call from Steven, and what he had found out from his call to the marina. "I may still be chasing ghosts," he said, "but everything points, to something going on here." She agreed, "It's looking more and more so." "Let's just say, for argument sake, they pulled a disappearing act. Could they stay in the U.S.? Their charges were dropped, so they would be protected by double jeopardy, right?" "Not really," she answered, "Double jeopardy doesn't play until the jury is sworn in at trial, or, in the case of a bench trial, when the first witness is called. The Comptons' were released at the preliminary hearing stage, so charges could be reinstated at any time, if new evidence was to come to light." "Well, what about charges in Canada, for say, a false kidnapping claim?" "If there was evidence of that, I'm certain the Crown would purse it." She said. "So all they would have to do, is lay low until the statute of limitations expired?" Jake suggested. Carla chuckled, "I think you may be watching too much television. Let me give you a crash course in law 101. In Canada, there is no statute of limitations for indictable offences, which in all probability, is how they would be charged. In the U.S., there would be a five-year limitation for a Federal crime, but only, if they were openly living a normal life in the community, which, like we just discussed, would leave them vulnerable to the U.S. charges being reinstated. Their only option would be to go into hiding, or, flee the country, which, in that case, there would be no limitation. They would also be subject to extradition back to Canada, if the Crown did purse charges." "So, bottom line is, if he was actually guilty of participating in his own kidnapping, the only real safety they're going to find, is in some country that doesn't have an extradition treaty, with Canada, or the U.S." Jake responded. "You have been paying attention." She said smiling. "I think that's worth pizza and a couple glasses of wine." Jake added. "Wait a minute he added, "the one additional thing we never considered, is the fact that Lyle Kohler isn't going to be in prison forever. He's out half a million dollars worth of drugs, and his only brother. The two governments may be the least of Frank and Margaret's problems." Carla just nodded in agreement. They finished eating, and to no surprise to either of them, found themselves at her place.

CHAPTER SEVENTEEN

Next morning, Jake was up early, and had a new energy within. The case was starting to show, that his instincts might have been right. He stopped by his own place to clean up, and grab a fresh change of clothes, before heading in to his office. After parking the car, Jake walked across the street, and ordered a breakfast bagel, and a large coffee to go, then went up to his office. He checked his phone messages. There were a couple of calls from potential clients he had met a couple of days ago, agreeing to his rate, and wanting to hire him. At ten o'clock, he called Steven.

He had decided to go at it, from the point of Lyle, possibly coming for restitution. When Steven answered, Jake told him, what he had found out, from his call to San Diego. "I know it's asking a lot, with privacy issues and all, but it might really help, if I could take a look at your dad's client files. There may be something in them to point us in the right direction." He said. "I don't know. I don't think dad would like us snooping around his clients personal financial information." "If anything happens to your parents, it's all a moot point. I'm certainly not going to divulge anything I find, unless it directly relates to locating your parents." "Ok," Steven agreed, "We'll meet at the house in an hour, and we'll go over them together." "Perfect, I'll see you then." Jake said, and then hung up. He felt bad working Steven like that, but didn't see any other way.

They both arrived at Frank's house at about the same time. Steven unlocked the front door, and they went inside. Jake stood in the living room, while Steven took a quick look around, to check on the place. Everything looked good, so they continued on to Frank's den, and started looking for his client files. Steven found the files they were looking for, in the top drawer of his filing cabinet. He pulled them out, and laid them on the desk. There were five. Just a quick look at each, was enough to eliminate them as being not relevant. One was the owner of a small music shop, another couple were independent sales reps, and the two remaining were similar types of businesses. Jakes heart sunk. He really believed he was on to something. Steven put the files back like they found them, and started to close the drawer. He had just about pushed it in all the way, when Jake said, "Stop!" A small corner of a manila folder could be seen sticking out of the underside of the drawer. Steven pulled it open all the way, and they took a look underneath. There was a single, manila file folder, duck-taped to the underside of the drawer. Jake carefully pulled it down, and opened the folder. There were two sheets of paper inside. The first page was a spreadsheet, with the words "LLK Holdings", typed at the top. "It had to mean Lyle and Leonard Kohler Holdings." the two men thought. Underneath was typed, "Cayman National", followed by a string of numbers. Below that, were the names and phone numbers, of what looked to be contacts. They both immediately knew what they were looking at. "Steve, do you still have the wire transfer information you used to wire the ransom money?" "Sure, I typed it into my cell phone as back up." He answered, as he pulled out his phone, and brought up the note. The first two groups of numbers were the same, but the last group was different. "It looks like the same bank, just different accounts." Jake suggested. "I would agree." Steven added. They flipped the first sheet over, and read what was on the second. It appeared to be a list of deposits, going back almost three years. When they looked at the total, Jake saw the color drain from Steven's face. "$3,800,000.00". He found a chair, and slumped down into it. "Ah dad, what the hell have you gotten yourself into?" Steven muttered, with total disappointment in his voice. "I'm so sorry Steven, I had my suspicions, but really couldn't say anything, until I had some tangible proof." "Well I'd say it doesn't get much more tangible than this." Steve answered. "I feel sick." "Look, all we know now, is that he was involved. We don't know to what degree, or why. You've known him all your life. Just by your reaction, I'm guessing this is totally out of character for him." "It is." Steven said, with a sigh. "I guess I owe him the benefit of the doubt, for now anyway." "You do." Jake agreed. "Let's go meet with Carla." Jake took photos of both pages with his cell phone, and they put everything back where they found it.

CHAPTER EIGHTEEN

Carla was expecting them. Jake had called her when they were on their way. All she knew, was that it was important. When they walked in the door, she was there to greet them. "Come straight on in. Can I offer you anything to drink?" She said as she led them. "Only if contains alcohol." Steven replied, only half joking. Without a word, she reached into a cabinet, and pulled out a bottle of scotch, and poured three glasses. "Water, anyone?" They were all good. "So, what's this all about?" she said looking back and forth at both of them. Jake relayed the afternoon's findings to her, showed her the document photos, and then asked, "Where do we go from here?"

"It depends on what end result are you looking to achieve?" Carla continued, "Your parents have obviously disappeared because they don't want to be found. I'm guessing, they're aware of the consequences, if they are brought back to Canada. I'm also assuming, they know that when Lyle is released, he'll be looking for his drugs, and especially, his money. They have some compelling reasons for staying in hiding. Even as their lawyer, I wouldn't be able to council them on how to evade law enforcement. The scenario I envision them doing, is taking refuge in a country that doesn't have extradition treaties, with Canada or the U.S. Someplace for example, like the Cayman Islands. That, after all, is where Frank has access to three point eight million dollars. The way I see it, is you have two options. One, you could spend, what I can only assume, would be a vast amount of time and money, trying to locate them. And, if you do succeed, then what? Do you really think they will come back with you? Second, leave it alone. Let them contact you, if and when, they are ready."

"Yes," Carla went on to say, "Frank not returning to Canada, would not serve justice, from the crown's point of view. But if his returning, resulted in a potential death sentence, at the hands of Lyle, would justice really be served? Sometimes it may be better when injustice is served.

For Steven there was really only one answer.

July 2015

(Postmark: San Diego, CA)

Dear Steven,

It is with great sorrow and embarrassment that I am writing this letter. You're a smart man, and I can only assume that by now, you have figured out a few things. I'm not trying to justify my actions, just explain them. I owe you and your family that much.

A few years ago, I took on a client. In the beginning, there was nothing unusual about the accounting work that I was doing for them. After a period of time, they asked me if I could arrange to open an off shore bank account for them. Again, not unusual, except that they wanted it done without the required government reports being filed. I know, at that point, I should have just walked away, but I didn't. They offered to pay me well above the usual fee for accounting services, and I took it. By the time I found out where the money was coming from, it was too late to back out. My involvement with their operation was strictly an administrative function, although admittedly an illegal one.

When the Kohler brothers realized the police had missed the drugs that they had squirrelled away in the sailboat, they asked me to buy the boat, when it went for auction. They reimbursed me for what I paid for the boat, plus promised me fifty thousand dollars, to deliver it to Friday Harbor. Who would suspect a couple of retired seniors? I was wrong, and now this is where we are. After you bailed us out of jail, I contacted Leonard and we devised the kidnapping plan. This would get your mom and me, off the hook with the smuggling charge, and get the Kohler's money back, for the lost drugs. I went along with it out of desperation.

I don't know when, or even If, we'll get to see you, and your family again. It's a far too expensive price to pay, for what I did. Be clear, that your mother had no idea of my actions, until we got back home from Washington. We have enough money to last us as long as it needs to. You have power of attorney over my affairs, so liquidate my assets as you see fit. They are all willed to you anyhow. Please don't attempt to find us, as it will only endanger us. We love you all, very much.

Love

Mom & Dad

THE END

This Page Intentionally Left Blank